# Passion Flower

# Passion Flower

## JEAN URE

Illustrated by Karen Donnelly

Collins

An imprint of HarperCollinsPublishers

*for Samantha and Stephanie Bond*

First published in Great Britain by Collins 2003
Collins is an imprint of HarperCollins*Publishers* Ltd,
77-85 Fulham Palace Road, Hammersmith,
London W6 8JB

The HarperCollins website address is
www.**fire**and**water**.com

1 3 5 7 9 8 6 4 2

Text copyright © Jean Ure 2003
Illustrations © Karen Donnelly 2003

ISBN 0 00 715619 7

The author and illustrator assert the moral right to be
identified as the author and illustrator of the work.

Printed and bound in England by
Clays Ltd, St Ives plc

# one

OF COURSE, MUM shouldn't have thrown the frying pan at Dad. Especially as it was full of oil, ready for frying. On the other hand, it wasn't as if it was hot. And it didn't even hit him. Mum is such a lousy shot! In any case, Dad deserved it.

Needless to say, the Afterthought didn't agree with me; she always took Dad's side. But I really didn't see what excuses could be made for him this time. Mum had been scrimping and saving for months to buy herself a new cooker. She had been ever so looking forward to it! It was really mean of Dad to go and gamble all the money away at the race track. I said this to the Afterthought, but she just said that it wasn't Dad's fault if his horse had come in last, and that if Mum didn't want him to spend the money why didn't she keep it in a separate account? I said, "Because they're *married*. Being married is about *sharing*." The Afterthought said in that case, Mum oughtn't to complain.

"Dad was only trying to make some money for us!"

I said, "He never makes money at the races."

"He does, too!" said the Afterthought. "What about that time he took us all out to dinner at that posh place and got champagne?"

"*Once*," I said. "He did it *once*. And anyway, Mum didn't want champagne."

"No, she wanted something boring, like a new cooker," said the Afterthought.

I have to admit that a new cooker would not come high on my list of priorities, but we are all different, and if Mum wanted a cooker I thought she ought to be allowed to have one. As she pointed out to Dad just before she threw the frying pan, she was the one who did all the cooking.

"You never lift a finger!"

"Why should he?" whined the Afterthought, when we were talking about it later. "Cooking's a woman's job!"

She doesn't really think that; she was only saying it to stick up for Dad. She was the most terrible daddy's girl.

Dad always hated it when Mum got mad at him. He would rush out and do these awful things that upset her, then grow all crestfallen and sorry for himself. That used to make Mum madder than ever! But somehow or other Dad always managed to get round her. He always promised that he wouldn't ever do it again. And Mum always believed him… until that day when he gambled away the money for her new cooker. That was what made her finally crack. She really blew her top!

"How am I expected to provide for a family of four on this clapped-out piece of junk?" screamed Mum.

I remember we all turned to look at the piece of junk. Half the burners had rotted away; one didn't work at all. The oven was unreliable. It kept burning things to crisps. Really annoying! Mum was absolutely right. But it didn't help when Dad, with a boyish grin at me and the Afterthought, suggested that we should all live on takeaways.

"Suit me! Wouldn't it suit you, girls?"

The Afterthought cried, "Yesss!"

Mum snapped, "Don't avoid the issue!" The issue being, I suppose, that Dad had gone and wasted all Mum's hard-earned money on a horse named Toasted Tea Cake that hadn't even reached the finishing point.

"Daniel Rose, you knew I was saving up for a new cooker!" screeched Mum.

That was when she reached for the frying pan. Dad backed away, holding his hands out in front of him.

"You can have a new cooker! You can have one!. We'll go out tomorrow and we'll get you one… heavens alive, woman! Haven't you ever heard of credit?"

That was when Mum *threw* the frying pan. We didn't buy things on credit any more; not since the car and the video got repossessed. We didn't even have a store card. Mum never did anything by halves. I guess I have to admit that she sometimes went to extremes. But it was Dad who pushed her! She'd probably have been quite normal if it hadn't been for him.

I don't know whether Dad was always the way he was. I mean, like, when he and Mum first met. I think from what Mum says he was just easygoing and fun. Dad *was* fun! He was more fun than Mum, but then it was Mum who had to look after us and provide for us and keep things going. Dad was really a bit of a walking disaster. He liked to say he was a free spirit, by which he meant that he couldn't be tied down to a regular job the same as other people, which meant he sometimes earned money but more often didn't, which meant it was all left to Mum, which was why she got so mad when he did some of the things that he did. Not just losing money on what he called "the gee-gees", but suddenly taking it into his head to go out and buy stuff that Mum said we couldn't afford and didn't need. Like, for instance, the time he came home with a camcorder. The camcorder was brilliant! Me and the Afterthought both sulked like crazy when it had to go back. And then there was the trampoline. That was pretty good, too! At least, it would have been if we'd had anywhere to put it. We tried it in the garden but our garden is about the size of a tea tray and the Afterthought bounced too high and fell into a prickly bush and screamed the place down. Mum said she could have poked an eye out, so that was the end of the trampoline.

These are just a few of the other things I remember Dad buying:

* a night owl light, so you could see in the dark (except that we never got around to using it as it came without batteries and Dad lost interest. Anything that came without batteries ended up in a drawer, forgotten).

* a microdot sleeping bag, in case one of us ever wanted to go off to camp. (The Afterthought tried sleeping out in the garden one night but got scared after

she'd been there about five minutes and had to come back indoors.)

* a digital car compass, which didn't work.

* an inflatable neck pillow, for Mum to use in the car. (It was supposed to give off soothing scents, only Mum said they made her feel sick. Even I thought that was a bit mean, after Dad had got it specially for her.)

* a digital watch camera (sent back before we could use it).

* a digital voice recorder (also sent back, more is the pity). and

* a special finger mouse for Dad's new laptop, which he said he needed for his work, whatever that was.

To be honest, I was never quite sure what work Dad actually did. When people at school asked me, like my best friend Vix Stephenson, I couldn't think what to say. Once when we were about ten Vix told me she had heard her mum saying that "What Stephanie's dad does is a total mystery." Vix asked me what it meant. Very quickly, I said, "It means that what he does is top secret." Vix's eyes grew wide.

"You mean, like... he's a spy, or something?"

I said, "Sort of."

"You mean he works for *MI5*?"

"I can't tell you," I said. "It's confidential."

It was so confidential I'm not sure that even Mum knew. 'Cos one time when I asked her she said, in this weary voice, that my guess was as good as hers. I said, "Mum, he's not a... a *criminal*, is he?"

It was something that had been worrying me. I had these visions of Dad climbing up drainpipes and going through windows and helping himself to stuff from people's houses. Tellies and videos and jewellery, and stuff. I didn't imagine him holding up petrol stations or anything like that; I didn't think he would ever be violent. Mum was the violent one, if anyone was! She was the one who threw things. But I was really scared that he might be a thief. I was quite relieved when Mum gave this short laugh and said, "Nothing so energetic! You have to have staying power for that... you have to be *organised*. That's the last thing you could accuse your dad of!" She said that Dad was an "opportunist".

"He just goes along for the ride."

I said, "You mean, he gets on trains without a ticket?"

"Something like that," said Mum.

"Oh, well! That's not so bad," I said.

"It's not so good, either," said Mum.

She sounded very bitter. I didn't like it when Mum sounded bitter. This was my dad she was talking about! My dad, who bought us trampolines and camcorders. Mum never bought us anything like that. I was still only little when we had this conversation, when I got worried in case Dad was a criminal; I mean, I was still at Juniors. I was in Year 8 by the time Mum threw the frying pan. I still loved Dad, I still hated it when Mum got bitter, but I was beginning to understand why she did. There were moments when I felt really sorry for Mum. She tried so hard! And just as she thought she'd got everything back on track, like paying off the arrears on the gas bill, or saving up for a new cooker, Dad would go and blow it all. He didn't mean to! It was like he just couldn't stop himself.

The day after Mum threw the frying pan, Dad left home. The Afterthought said that Mum got rid of him, and I think for once she may have been right. Mum was certainly very fed up. She said that Dad spending her cooker money was the last straw.

I don't think that she and Dad had a row; at any rate, I never heard any sounds of shouting. I think she simply told him to go, and he went. He was there when we left for school in the morning – and gone by the time we got back. Mum sat us down at the kitchen table and broke the news to us.

"Your dad and I have decided to live apart. You'll still see him – he's still your dad – but we're just not going to be living together any more. It's best for all of us."

Well! Mum may have thought it was best, but me and the Afterthought were stunned. How could Dad leave us, just like that? Without any warning? Without even saying goodbye?

"It was Mum," sobbed the Afterthought. "She threw him out!"

That was what Dad said, too, when he rang us later that same evening. He said, "Well, kids —" we were both listening in, me on the extension "– it looks like this is it for your poor old dad. Given my marching orders! Seems I've upset her Royal Highness just once too often. Now she won't have me in the house any more."

Dad was trying to make light of it, 'cos that was Dad. He was always joking and fooling around, he never took anything seriously. But I could tell he was quite shaken. I don't think he ever dreamt that Mum would really throw him out. Always, in the past, he'd managed to get round her. They'd kiss and make up, and Mum would end up laughing, in spite of herself, and saying that Dad was shameless. But not this time! This time, he'd really blown it.

"She's had enough of me," said Dad. "She doesn't love me any more."

"Dad, I'm sure she does!" I said.

"She doesn't, Steph. She told me… *Daniel Rose, I've had it with you. You get out of my life once and for all.* Those were her words. That's what she said to me. *I've had it with you.*"

Oh, Dad, I thought, stop! I can't bear it!

"She's a cow!" shrieked the Afterthought, all shrill.

"No, Sam. Never say that about your mum. She's had a lot to put up with."

"So have you!" shrieked the Afterthought.

"Ah, well… I've probably deserved it," said Dad. He was being ever so meek about it all. Taking the blame, not letting us say anything bad about Mum. Meek wasn't like my dad! But that, somehow, just made it all the worse, what she'd done to him.

"Dad, what are you going to do?" I said.

"I don't know, Steph, and that's a fact. I'm a bit shaken up just at the moment. Got to get my act together."

"Shall I try asking Mum if she'll let you come back?"

"Better hadn't. Only set her off again."

"But you don't *want* to go, do you, Dad?"

"*Want* to? What do you think?" said Dad. "Go and leave my two girls? It's breaking my heart, Pusskin!"

He had me crying, in the end. If he'd been spitting blood, like Mum, I wouldn't have felt quite so bad about it. I mean, I'd still have felt utterly miserable at the thought of him not being with us, but at least I'd have understood that he and Mum just couldn't go on living together any more. But Dad still thought Mum was the bee's knees! It's what he'd always called her: the bee's knees. *He* wasn't the one that wanted to break up. It was Mum who was ruining everything.

"Couldn't you just give him one last chance?" I begged.

"Stephanie, I have lost count of all the last chances I've given that man," said Mum. "I'm sorry, but enough is enough. He has turned my life into turmoil!"

It is very upsetting, when one of your parents suddenly isn't there any more; it's like a big black hole. The poor old Afterthought took it very hard. She went into a crying fit that lasted for days, and when she couldn't cry any more she started on the sulks. No one can sulk like the Afterthought! Mum tried everything she

knew. She coaxed and cajoled, she cuddled and kissed –
as best she could, with the Afterthought fighting her off
– until in the end she lost patience and snapped, "It
hasn't been easy for me, you know, all these years!" The
Afterthought just went on sulking.

Mum said, "Stephanie, for goodness' sake talk to her!
We can't carry on like this."

I tried, but the Afterthought said she wasn't going to
forgive Mum, *ever*. She said if she couldn't be with Dad,
her life wasn't worth living.

"Why couldn't I go with him?"

I suggested this to Mum, but Mum tightened her lips
and said, "No way! Your father wouldn't even be capable
of looking after a pot plant."

"It's not up to her!" screamed the Afterthought. "It's
up to me! I'm old enough! I can choose who I want to
be with!"

But when she asked Dad, the next time he rang us, Dad said that much as he would love to have the Afterthought with him – "and your sister, too!" – it just wasn't possible right at this moment.

"He's got to get settled," said the Afterthought. "As soon as he's settled, I can go and live with him!"

"Over my dead body," said Mum.

"I can!" screeched the Afterthought. "I'm old enough! You can't stop me! As soon as he's settled!"

Even I knew that the chances of Dad getting settled were about zilch; Dad just wasn't a settling kind of person. But it seemed to make the Afterthought happy. She seemed to think she'd scored over Mum. Whenever Mum did anything to annoy her she'd shriek, "It won't be like this when I go and live with Dad!" Or if Mum wouldn't let her have something she wanted, it was, "Dad would let me!" There was, like, this permanent feud between the Afterthought and Mum.

Her name isn't really the Afterthought, by the way. Not that I expect anyone ever thought it was. Even flaky people like Dad don't christen their children with names like Afterthought, and anyway, Mum would never have let him. Her name is actually Samantha; but I once asked Mum and Dad why they'd waited four years between us, instead of having us quickly, one after the other, so that we'd be nearer the same age and could be friends and do things together and talk the same language (instead of one of us being almost grown up and the other a *child*, and quite a tiresome one, at that). Mum said it was because they hadn't really been going to have any more kids. She said, "Sam was an afterthought." Dad at once added, "But a very nice afterthought! We wouldn't want to be without her."

Oh, no? Well, I suppose we wouldn't. She's all right, really; just a bit young. Hopefully she'll grow out of it. Anyway, that was when me and Dad started calling her the Afterthought. Just as a joke, to begin with, but then it sort of stuck. Mum never called her that. The Afterthought said she wouldn't want her to.

"It's Dad's name for me!"

I wasn't sure how I felt when Dad left home. I mean, like, once I'd got over the first horrible shock. I did miss him terribly, but I also had some sympathy with Mum. Mum and me had done some talking, and I could see that Dad had really made things impossible for her. So that while feeling sorry for poor old Dad, thrown out on his ear, I did on the whole tend to side with Mum. Like I would always stick up for her when the Afterthought accused her of turning Dad out on to the street – 'cos Dad had told us that he had nowhere to go and might have to live in a shop doorway. To which Mum just said, "Huh! A likely tale. He'll always land on his feet." The Afterthought said that Mum was cruel, and I suppose she did sound a bit hard, but I still stuck up for her. Then one day, when Dad had been gone for about two weeks, I told Vix about it, because, I mean, she was my best friend, and she had to know, you can't keep things from your best friend, and Vix said, "It's horrid when people's mum and dad split up, but I'm sure it's all for the best. My mum's always said she doesn't know how your mum put up with it for so long."

I froze when she said this. I said, "Put up with *what*?"

"Well… your dad," said Vix. "You know?" She muttered it, apologetically. "The things he did."

I said, "How do you know what things he did?"

Vix said she'd heard her mum talking about it.

I said, "How did *she* know?"

"Your mum told her," said Vix.

Suddenly, that made me lose all sympathy with Mum. Talking about Dad to other people! To *strangers*. Well, outsiders. I thought that was so disloyal!

"Steph, I'm sorry," said Vix.

I told her that it wasn't her fault. It was Mum's fault, if anyone's. How could she do such a thing?

"Dad wasn't as bad as all that," I said. "He never did anything on purpose to hurt her! He *loved* her."

Vix looked at me, pityingly.

"Well, but he did!" I said. "He couldn't help it if he wasn't very good at earning money… money just didn't mean anything to him."

"I suppose that's why he spent it," said Vix.

She wasn't being sarcastic; she was genuinely trying to help.

"He spent it because he wanted Mum to have nice things," I said. "Not stupid, boring things like cookers!"

"But perhaps she wanted stupid boring things," said Vix.

"Well, she did," I said, "but Dad wasn't to know! I mean, he *did* know, but – he kept forgetting. He'd see something he thought she'd like, and he couldn't resist getting it for her. And then she'd say it was a waste of money, or stupid, or useless, or she'd make him take it back... poor Dad! He was only trying to make her happy."

"This is it," said Vix.

What did she mean, *this is it*?

"It's what people do," said Vix. "When they're married... they try to make each other happy, but sometimes it doesn't always work and they just make each other miserable, and – and they only get happy when they're not living together any more. Maybe," she added.

Mum ought to have been happier, now she'd got rid of Dad and could save up for new cookers without any fear of him gambling her money away on horses that didn't reach the finishing point. You'd have *thought* she'd be happier. Instead, she just got crabbier and crabbier, even worse than she'd been before, when Dad was turning her life into turmoil. At least, that's how it seemed to me and the Afterthought. She wouldn't let us do things, she wouldn't let us have things, she wouldn't let us buy the clothes we wanted, we couldn't even *read* what we wanted.

"This magazine is disgusting!" cried Mum, slapping down my latest copy of *Babe*. *Babe* just happened, at the time, to be my favourite teen mag. I've grown out of it now; but at the age of thirteen there were things I desperately needed to know, and *Babe* was where I found out about them.

I mean, you have to find out *somewhere*. You can't go through life being ignorant.

I tried explaining this to Mum but she had frothed herself up into one of her states and wouldn't listen.

"*DO BLOKES PREFER BOOBS OR BUMS?* At *your* age?"

"Mum," I said, "I need to know!"

"You'll find out quite soon enough," said Mum, "without resorting to this kind of trash... what, for heaven's sake, is *Daddy drool* supposed to mean?"

Again, I tried explaining: "It means when people fancy your dad." But again she wouldn't listen.

"This is just so cheap! It is just so *tacky*! Where did you get it from?"

I said, "The newsagent."

"Mr Patel? I'm surprised he'd sell you such a thing!"

"Mum, *everybody* reads it," I said.

"Does Victoria read it?" said Mum.

I said, "No, she reads one that's even worse." I giggled. "Then we swop!"

It was a mistake to giggle. Mum immediately thought that I was cheeking her. Plus she'd actually gone and opened the mag and her eye had fallen on a rather *cheeky* article (ha ha, that is a joke!) about male bums. Shock, horror! Did she think I'd never seen one before???

"For crying out loud!" Mum glared at the offending article, bug-eyed. Maybe *she'd* never seen one before... "What is this? Teenage porn?"

I said, "Mum, it's just facts of life."

"So is sewage," said Mum.

Was she saying male bums were *sewage*? No! She'd flicked over the page and seen something else.

Something I'd been really looking forward to reading!

"This is unbelievable," said Mum. "Selling this stuff to thirteen-year-old girls! I'm going to have a word with Mr Patel."

"Mum! No!" I shrieked.

I wasn't worried about Mr Patel, I was worried about *Babe*. How was I going to learn things if he wasn't allowed to sell it to me any more?

"Stephanie, I don't want this kind of filth in the house," said Mum. "Do you understand?"

I sulkily said yes, while thinking to myself that I bet Dad wouldn't have minded. Mum had just got *so crabby*.

"She's an old cow," said the Afterthought.

Mum and the Afterthought were finding it really difficult to get along; they rowed even worse than Mum and me. The Afterthought wanted a kitten. A girl in her class had a cat that was going to have some, and the Afterthought had conceived this passion. (Conceived!

Ha! What would Mum say to *that*?) Every day the Afterthought nagged and begged and howled and pleaded; and every day Mum very firmly said *no*. She said she was sorry, but she had quite enough to cope with without having an animal to look after.

"Kittens grow into cats, and cats need feeding, cats need injections, cats cost money... I'm sorry, Sam! It's just not the right moment. Maybe in a few months."

"That'll be too late!" wailed the Afterthought. "All the kittens will be gone!"

"There'll be more," said Mum.

"Not from Sukey. They won't be *Sukey's* kittens. I want one of Sukey's! She's so sweet. Dad would let me!" roared the Afterthought.

"Very possibly, but your dad doesn't happen to be here," said Mum.

"No! Because you got rid of him! *I want my kitten!*" bellowed the Afterthought.

It ended up, as it always did, with Mum losing patience and the Afterthought going off into one of her tantrums. I told Vix that life at home had become impossible. Vix said, "Yes, for me, too! Specially after your mum talked to my mum about teenage filth and now my mum says I'm not to buy that sort of thing any more!" I stared at her, appalled.

"What right have they got," I said, "to talk about us behind our backs?"

The weeks dragged on, with things just going from bad to worse. Mum got crabbier and crabbier. She got specially crabby on days when we had telephone calls from Dad. He rang us, like, about once every two weeks, and the Afterthought always snatched up the phone and grizzled into it.

"Dad, it's horrible here! When are you going to get settled?"

I tried to be a *little* bit more discreet, because I could see that probably it was a bit irritating for Mum. I mean, she was doing her best. Dad was now living down south, in Brighton. He said that he missed us and would love to have us with him, but he wasn't quite settled enough; not just yet.

"Soon, I hope!"

Triumphantly, the Afterthought relayed this to Mum. "Soon Dad's going to be settled, and then we can go and live with him!"

I knew that Mum would never let us, and in any case I wasn't really sure that I'd want to. Not permanently, I mean. I loved Dad to bits, because he wasn't ever crabby like Mum, I couldn't remember Dad telling us off for anything, ever; but I couldn't imagine actually leaving Mum, no matter how impossible she was being. And she *was* being. Running off to Vix's mum like that! Interfering with Vix's life, as well as mine. I didn't think she ought to have done that; it could have caused great problems between me and Vix. Fortunately Vix

25

understood that it wasn't my fault. As she said, "You can't control how your mum behaves." But Vix's mum had been quite put out to discover that her angelic daughter was reading about s.e.x. and gazing at pictures of male bums. It's what comes of living in a grungy old place way out in the sticks where nothing ever happens and s.e.x. is something you are not supposed to have heard of, let alone think about. Vix agreed with me that in Brighton people probably thought about it all the time, even thirteen-year-old girls, and no one turned a hair.

I said to Mum, "When I am *fourteen*," (which I was going to be quite soon), "can I think about it then?"

"You can think about it all you like," said Mum. "I just don't want you reading about it in trashy magazines. That's all!"

It was shortly after my fourteenth birthday that Mum finally went and flipped. I'd been trying ever so hard to make allowances for her. I'd discussed it with Vix and we had agreed that it was probably something to do with her age. Vix said, "Women get really odd when they reach a certain age. How old *is* your mum?"

I said, "She's only thirty-six." I mean, pretty old, but not actually decrepit.

"Old enough," said Vix. "She's probably getting broody."

I said, "Getting *what*?"

"Broody. You know?"

"I thought that was something to do with chickens," I said.

"Chickens and women… it makes them desperate."

"Desperate for what?"

"Having babies while they still can."

"But she's had babies!" I said.

"Doesn't make any difference," said Vix. "Don't worry! She'll grow out of it."

"Yes, but *when*?" I wailed.

"Dunno." Vix wrinkled her nose. "When she's about … fifty, maybe?"

I thought that fifty was a long time to wait for Mum to stop being desperate, but in the meanwhile, in the interests of peaceful living, I would do my best to humour her. I would no longer read nasty magazines full of s.e.x., at any rate, not while I was indoors, and I would no longer nag her for new clothes except when I really, really needed them, and I would make my bed and I would tidy my bedroom and I would help with the washing up, and do all those things that she was always on at me to do. So I did. *For an entire whole week.* And then she went and flipped! All because I'd been to a party and got home about *two seconds* later than she'd said. Plus I'd just happened to be brought back by this boy that for some reason she'd taken exception to and told me not to see any more, only I hadn't realised that she meant it. I mean, how was I to know that she'd meant it?

"What did you think I meant?" said Mum, all cold and brittle, like an icicle. "I told you I didn't want you seeing him any more!"

"But why not?" I said. "What's the matter with him?"

"Stephanie, we have already been through all this," said Mum.

"But it doesn't make any sense! He's just a boy, the same as any other boy. It's not like he's on drugs, or anything."

Well, he wasn't; not as far as I knew. It's stupid to think that just because someone has a nose stud and tattoos he's doing drugs. Mum was just so prejudiced! But I suppose I shouldn't have tried arguing with her; I can see, now, that that was a bit ill-judged. Mum went up like a light. She went *incandescent.* Fire practically spurted out of her nostrils. I couldn't ever remember seeing her that mad. And at *me*! Who'd tried her best to make allowances! It didn't help that the Afterthought was there, leaning over the banisters. The Afterthought never can manage to keep her mouth shut. She had to go starting on about kittens again.

"Dad would have let me have one! You never let us have anything! You're just a misery! You aren't any *fun*!"

She said afterwards that she thought she was coming to my aid. She thought she was being supportive.

"Showing that I was on your side!"

All it did, of course, was make matters worse. Mum just suddenly snapped. She raised two clenched fists to heaven and demanded to know what she had done to get lumbered with two such beastly brats.

"Thoroughly unpleasant! Totally ungrateful! Utterly selfish! Well, that's it. I've had it! I'm sick to death of the pair of you! As far as I'm concerned, your father can have you, and welcome. I've done my stint. From now on, you can be his responsibility!"

Wow. I think even the Afterthought was a bit taken aback.

# two

"I HAVE SPENT sixteen years of my life," said Mum, "coping with your dad. Sixteen years of clearing up his messes, getting us out of the trouble that he's got us into. If it weren't for me, God alone knows where this family would be! Out on the streets, with a begging bowl. Well, I've had it, do you hear? I have *had it.* I cannot take any more! Do I make myself plain?"

Me and the Afterthought, shocked into silence, just stared woodenly.

"Do I make myself plain?" bellowed Mum.

"Y-yes!" I snapped to attention. "Absolutely!"

"Good. Then you will understand why it is that I am

relinquishing all responsibility. Because if I am asked to cope just one minute longer –" Mum's voice rose to a piercing shriek "– with your tempers and your tantrums and your utter – your utter—"

We waited.

"Your utter *selfishness*," screamed Mum, "I shall end up in a lunatic asylum! Have you got that?"

I nodded.

"I said, *have you got that*?" bawled Mum.

"Got it," I said.

"Got it," muttered the Afterthought.

"Right! Just so long as you have. I want there to be no misunderstandings. Now, get off to bed, the pair of you!"

Me and the Afterthought both scuttled into our bedrooms and stayed there. I wondered gloomily if Mum was having a nervous breakdown, and if so, whether it was my fault. All I'd done was just go to a party! I lay awake the rest of the night thinking that if Mum ended up in a lunatic asylum, I would be the one that put her there, but when I told Vix about it next day Vix said that me going to the party was probably just the last straw. She said that her mum had said that my mum had been under pressure for far too long.

"She's probably cracking up," said Vix.

Honestly! Vix may be my best and oldest friend, but I can't help feeling she doesn't always stop and think before she opens her mouth. *Cracking up*. What a

thing to say! It worried me almost sick. I crept round
Mum like a little mouse, hardly daring even to breathe
for fear of upsetting her. I had these visions of her
suddenly tearing off all her clothes and running naked
into the street and having to be locked up. The
Afterthought, being almost totally
insensitive where other people's
feelings are concerned, just
carried on the same as
usual, except that she
didn't actually whinge
quite as much. Instead
of whining about
cornflakes for breakfast
instead of sugar puffs, for
instance, she simply rolled
her eyes and made huffing
sounds; instead of screaming
that "Dad would let me!"
when Mum refused to
let her sit up till

midnight watching telly, she just did this angry scoffing
thing, like "Khuurgh!" and walloped out of the room,
slamming the door behind her.

I, in the meantime, was on eggshells, waiting for
Mum to tear her clothes off. In fact she didn't. After her
one manic outburst, she became deadly cool and calm,

which was quite frightening in itself as I felt that underneath *things were bubbling*. Like it would take just one little incident and that would be it: clothes off, running naked. Or, alternatively, tearing out her hair in great chunks, which is what I'd read somewhere that people did when they were having breakdowns.

I told the Afterthought to stop being so horrible. "You don't want Mum to end up in a lunatic asylum, do you?" The Afterthought just tossed her head and said she couldn't care less.

"I hate her! I'll always hate her! She sent my dad away!"

"*Your* dad? He's my dad, too!" I said.

"I'm the one that loves him best! You can have *her*," said the Afterthought. "She's your favourite!"

One week later, term came to an end. *The very next day*, Mum got rid of us. Well, that was what it seemed like. Like she just couldn't wait to be free. She'd made us pack all our stuff the night before, but she couldn't actually ship us off until after lunch as Dad said he had to work. Mum said, "On a *Saturday*?" She was fuming! Now she'd made up her mind to dump us, she wanted us to go *now*, at once, immediately. The Afterthought would have liked to go now, at once, immediately, too. She was jigging with impatience the whole morning. I sort of wanted to go – I mean, I was really looking forward to seeing Dad again – but I still couldn't quite believe that Mum was doing this to us.

As we piled into the car with all our gear, I said, "It's just for the summer holidays, right?"

Well, it had to be! I mean, what about clothes? What about school?

"I wouldn't want to miss any school," I said.

"Really?" said Mum. "I never heard that one before!"

OK, I knew she was still mad at us, but I didn't see there was any need for sarcasm. I said, "Well, but anyway, you'll be back long before then!"

Mum had announced that she was flying off to Spain to stay with an old school friend who owned a nightclub. She'd said she was going to "live it up". It worried me because I didn't think of Mum as a living-it-up kind of person. I couldn't imagine her drinking and dancing and lying about on the beach.

How would she cope? It just wasn't *Mum*.

"You'll have to be back," I said.

"Will I?" said Mum. "Why?"

*Why*? What kind of a question was that?

"You have to *work*," I said.

Mum had this job in the customer service department of one of the big stores in the centre of Nottingham. She had responsibilities. She couldn't just disappear for months!

"Actually," said Mum, "I don't have to work... I jacked it in. I've left."

I said, "*What?*"

"I've left," said Mum. "I gave in my notice."

"Gave in your *notice*?" I was aghast. Mum couldn't do that!

"You can't!" I bleated.

"I have," said Mum. "I gave it in last week... I'm unemployed!"

I shrieked, "*Mum!*"

"What's the problem?" said Mum. "It never seemed to bother you when your dad was unemployed."

"That was because he couldn't be tied down," said the Afterthought, in angry tones.

"Well, I've decided... neither can I!" Mum giggled. I don't think I'd ever heard Mum giggle before. "Two can play at being free spirits."

"But what will we live on?" I wailed.

"Ah!" said Mum. "That's the question... what will we live on? Worrying, isn't it? Maybe your dad will provide."

I glanced at the Afterthought. Her lip was quivering. She wanted to be with Dad OK, but only so long as Mum was still there, in the background, like a kind of safety net. We couldn't have two parents being free spirits!

"As a matter of fact," said Mum, "I'm thinking of going in with Romy."

I said, "*Romy?*"

"Yes!" said Mum. "Why not? Do you have some objection?"

"You're not going to *marry* him?" I said.

"Did I say I was going to marry him?"

I said, "N-no. But—"

"She couldn't, anyway!" shrilled the Afterthought. "She's still married to Dad!"

Yes, I thought, but for how long? I remembered when Vix's mum and dad split up. Vix had been *so sure* they would never get divorced, but now her dad was married to someone else and had a new baby. I didn't want that happening with my mum and dad! And the thought of having Je*rome* as a stepfather... yeeurgh! He has ginger hairs up his nose.

"Don't get yourselves in a lather," said Mum. "It's purely a business arrangement." Dreamily, she added, "I've always been interested in antiques."

"Romy doesn't sell antiques!" said the Afterthought, scornfully. "He sells junk. Dad says so!"

I said, "Shut up, you idiot!" But the damage had been done. We drove the rest of the way to the station in a very frosty silence. Mum parked the car in frosty silence. We marched across the forecourt with our bags and our backpacks in the same frosty silence. I thought, this is horrible! We weren't going to see Mum again for weeks and weeks. I didn't want to leave her all hurt and angry. Mum obviously felt the same, for she suddenly hugged me and said, "Look after yourself! Take care of your sister."

I promised that I would. The prospect didn't exactly thrill me, since quite honestly the Afterthought, in those days, was nothing but one big pain. She really *was* a beastly brat. But Mum was going off to Spain, and I was starting to miss her already, and I desperately, desperately didn't want us to part on bad terms. So I said, "I'll take care of her, Mum!" and Mum gave me a quick smile and a kiss and I felt better than I had in a long time. She then turned to the Afterthought and said, "Sam?" in this pleading kind of voice, which personally I didn't think she should have used. I mean, the Afterthought was behaving like total scum. For a moment I thought the horrible brat was going to stalk off without saying goodbye, but then, in grumpy fashion, she offered her cheek for a kiss.

We settled ourselves on the train, with various magazines that Mum had bought for us (*Babe*, unfortunately, not being one of them).

"Mum," I said, "you will be all right, won't you?"

"I'll be fine," said Mum. "Don't you worry about me! You just concentrate on having a good time, because that's what I'm going to do. And you, Sam, I want you to behave yourself! Do what your sister tells you and don't give her any trouble."

I smirked: the Afterthought pulled a face. As the train pulled out, Mum called after us: "Enjoy yourselves! Have fun. I'm sure you will!"

"I'm going to have *lots* of fun," boasted the Afterthought. "It's always fun with Dad!" She then added, "And you needn't think you're going to boss me around!"

"You've got to do what I tell you," I said. "Mum said so."

"Mum won't be there! So sah sah sah!"

The Afterthought pulled a face and stuck out her tongue. *So* childish. I turned to look out of the window.

Why was it, I thought, that our family always seemed to be at war? Mum and Dad, me and the Afterthought…

"It's like the Wars of the Roses," I said.

"What is?" said the Afterthought.

"Us! Fighting! The Wars of the Roses." Personally I thought this was rather clever, but the Afterthought didn't seem to get it. She just scowled and said, "It's Mum's fault."

She really had it in for Mum. She wouldn't hear a word against Dad, but everything that Mum did was wrong. Even now, when we weren't going to be seeing her for months. Poor old Mum!

Actually I couldn't help feeling that Mum and the Afterthought were quite alike. Neither of them ever did anything by halves. They were both so *extreme*. I like to think I am a bit more flexible, like Dad. Only more organised, naturally!

I tried to organise the Afterthought, on our trip down to London. It was quite a long journey, nearly two hours, so Mum had given us food packs in case we got hungry. I told the Afterthought she wasn't to start eating until we were halfway there, but she said she would eat when she wanted, and she broke open her pack right there and then and had scoffed the lot by the time we reached Bedford.

"You're not going to have any of mine," I said.

"Don't want any of yours," said the Afterthought. "We'll be in London soon and Dad will take us for tea."

This was what he had promised. He was going to be there at St Pancras station to meet us, and we were all going to go and have tea before we got on the train to Brighton. I had never made such a long train journey all by myself before. It was quite a responsibility, what with having to keep an eye on the Afterthought and make sure she didn't wander off and get lost, or lock herself in the toilet, or something equally stupid. But I didn't really mind. Now that we were on our way, I found I was quite excited at the prospect of staying with Dad. I'd never been to Brighton. I'd only been to London once, and that was a school trip, when we went to visit a museum. School trips are fun, and better than being in school, but you are still watched all the time and never allowed to go off and do your own thing, in case, I suppose, you get abducted or find a boy and run away with him. *I wish!*

I didn't think that Dad

would watch us; he is not at all a mother hen type. And Brighton sounded like a really wild and wicked kind of place! Vix had informed me excitedly that "things happen in Brighton". When I asked her what things, she didn't seem too sure, but she said that it was "a hub". Nottingham isn't a hub; well, I don't think it is. And *outside* of Nottingham is like living in limbo. Just nothing ever happens at all. Vix had made me promise to send her postcards every week and to email her if I met any boys. I intended to! Meet boys, that is. Mum, meanwhile, said that Brighton was "just the sort of place I would expect your dad to end up in." She said that it was cheap, squalid and tacky. Sounded good to me!

Just after we left Bedford (and the Afterthought finished off her supply of food) my mobile rang. It was Mum, checking that we were still on the train and hadn't got off at the wrong station or fallen out of the window, though as a matter of fact the windows were sealed, so that even the Afterthought couldn't have fallen out.

"Stephie?" said Mum. "Everything OK?"

I said, "Yes, fine, Mum. The Afterthought's eaten all her food."

"Well, that's all right," said Mum. "I'm sure your dad will get her some more. Don't forget to give him the cheque. Tell him it's got to last you."

I said, "Yes, Mum."

"Tell him it's for you and Sam. For your personal spending."

"*Yes*, Mum."

"I don't want him using it for himself."

"*No*, Mum." We had already been through all this! Plus I had heard Mum telling Dad on the phone.

"Oh, and Stephanie," she said.

"Yes, Mum?"

"I want you to ring me when you've arrived."

"What, in London?" I said.

"No! In Brighton. When you get to your dad's place. All right?"

I said, "Yes, Mum." I thought, "Mum's getting cold feet!" She'd gone and packed us off and now she was starting to do her mumsy thing, worrying in case something happened. I said, "We're only going to *Brighton*, Mum! Not Siberia."

"Yes, well, just look after your sister," said Mum.

"I've got to *look after you*," I said to the Afterthought.

"I don't want to be looked after," said the Afterthought.

We reached London nearly ten minutes late, so I expected Dad to already be there, waiting for us. But he wasn't! We stood at the barrier, looking all around, and he just wasn't there.

"Maybe he's gone to the loo," said the Afterthought, doing her best to sound brave.

"Mm," I said. "Maybe."

Or maybe we were looking in the wrong place. Maybe when Dad had said he'd meet us at St Pancras, he'd meant... *outside*. So we went and looked outside, but he wasn't there, either, so then we went back to where the train had come in. Still no sign of Dad.

"He must have been held up," I said. "We'd better just wait."

"Ring him!" said the Afterthought. "Ring him, Stephie, *now*!"

"Oh! Yes, I could, couldn't I?" I said. I called up Dad's number, but nothing happened. "He must have switched his phone off," I said.

"Why would he do that?" said the Afterthought, fretfully.

"I don't know! Maybe he's... in a tunnel, or something, and it's not working."

The Afterthought was already sucking her thumb and looking tearful. I thought that if Dad hadn't arrived by four o'clock I would have to ring Mum. Ringing Mum was the last thing I wanted to do! She would instantly start fretting and fuming and saying how Dad couldn't be trusted and she should never have let us go.

She might even tell us to jump on the first train home. How could I face Vix if I ended up back in Nottingham without having gone anywhere?

I was still dithering when my own phone rang, and there was Dad on the other end. Relief! I squealed, "Dad!" and the Afterthought immediately attempted to snatch the phone away from me. I kept her off with my elbow.

"Stephie?" said Dad. "That you?"

I said, "Yes, we're at St Pancras. I tried to call you but I couldn't get through!"

"No, I know," said Dad. "The thing's stopped working, I think it needs a new battery. Now listen, honeysuckle, you're going to have to make your own way down to Brighton. I've been a bit tied up, business-wise, and I couldn't get away. I'll meet you at Brighton, instead. OK?"

I gulped and said, "Y-yes, I s-suppose. But I don't know how to get there!"

"Not to worry," said Dad. "I'll give you directions."

Dad told me that we had to *turn left* out of St Pancras and follow the signs to the *Thameslink*. Then all we had to do was get on a train that said Brighton.

"Nothing to it! Think you can manage?"

What I actually thought was *no*! But I said yes because it didn't seem like I had any alternative. I mean, if I had said no, what was Dad supposed to do about it?

"He could have come and fetched us," whimpered the Afterthought.

"That would take for ever," I said. "Just stop being such a baby! There's nothing to it."

It was, however, quite scary. There were so many people about! All going places. All in such a *rush*. Also, just at first I couldn't see any signs that said Thameslink, and then when I did I couldn't make out which road we had to go down and had to ask someone. That was quite scary in itself because St Pancras station is right next door to King's Cross, and I had heard bad things about King's Cross. I had heard it was where all the prostitutes were, and the drug dealers, and the child molesters. I mean, they probably didn't come out until late at night, under cover of darkness, but you just never know. I didn't want us being abducted! Fortunately the person I spoke to (while I held tightly on to the Afterthought's hand in case they tried to snatch her) didn't seem to be any of those things, but just told us which road to take and went on her way.

I said, "Phew!" and tried to unhook myself from the Afterthought's hand, which had become rather hot and clammy, but the Afterthought went on clutching like mad.

"I don't like this place!" she said.

I said, "Neither do I, that's why we're getting out of it. Just come *on*!" And I dragged her all the way down the road until we came to the Thameslink station where an Underground man (he was wearing uniform, so I knew he was all right) told us which platform to go to. I felt quite pleased with myself. I felt quite proud! Dad had trusted me to get us on the right train, and I had. Mum wouldn't have trusted me. She still treated me as if I were about ten years old. (Not letting me read my magazine!) Dad was prepared to treat me like I was almost grown up. He knew I could handle it. I liked that!

Now that I had got us safely under way and hadn't let her be abducted, the Afterthought had gone all bumptious and full of herself again. She went off to the buffet car and came back with a fizzy drink which she slurped noisily and disgustingly through a straw. It really got on my nerves. I was trying to behave like a civilised human being, for heaven's sake! I was trying to have a bit of *style*. I didn't need this underage mutant showing me up. I tried telling her to suck *quietly*, but she immediately started slurping worse than ever. I mean, she did it quite deliberately. Defying me.

"Did you know," I said, "that your teeth have gone all purple?"

"So what?" said the Afterthought.

"So they'll probably stay like it… you'll probably be stained for life!"

I thought it might at least shut her up, but she just pulled her lips into this hideous grimace and started chittering like a monkey. *Well* over the top. In the end I moved to the other side of the carriage and let her get on with it. At least I didn't have to hold her horrible sticky hand any more.

Dad was waiting for us when we got to Brighton. I was so pleased to see him! He was looking just *fan*tastic. He had this deep, dark tan, and his hair had grown quite long. Dad's hair is very black, and curly. It suited him long! I could suddenly understand how Mum had fallen for him, all those years ago. I could understand how it was that he could always get round her, and make

her believe that this time things were going to be different, that he had mended his ways, he was going to behave himself. Dad wasn't capable of behaving himself! Once when Mum was in a good mood, I remember she said that he was "a lovable rogue". (More often, of course, she was in a bad mood, and threw things.)

"Dad!" I galloped up the platform towards him.

"Girls!" Dad threw open his arms and we both hurled ourselves into them. "Oh, girls!" cried Dad. "I've missed you!"

I thought, this is going to be the best holiday *ever*.

# three

THE FIRST THING we did was go back to Dad's place to dump our bags. Very earnestly, with her hand tucked into Dad's, the Afterthought said, "I'm glad you didn't have to go and live in a cardboard box. I was really worried about that."

Dad said, "Were you, poppet? That's sweet of you. I bet your mum wasn't!"

"I think she was," I said.

"She wasn't!" said the Afterthought. "She didn't care!"

I said, "She did! But she thought you'd be all right, because she said you always landed on your feet."

"Oh, did she?" said Dad. "And I suppose she thinks that you don't have to work, to land on your feet. I suppose she thinks it just happens?"

I didn't know what to say to that.

"Why are we talking about Mum?" shrilled the Afterthought.

"Good question," said Dad. "Your mum's gone off to Spain to enjoy herself, we'll enjoy ourselves in Brighton. Let's get shot of these bags, then we can go out and paint the town!"

Dad was living in a tiny little narrow street near to the station. The houses were little and narrow, too. All tastefully painted in pinks and lemons and greens, with their doors opening right on to the pavement.

"Oh! They're so *sweet*," crooned the Afterthought. "Like little dolls' houses!"

"Better than a cardboard box, eh?" said Dad.

Better than the house we had at home! Our house at home was on an estate that belonged to the Council, and wasn't very nice. I mean, it was actually quite ugly. Mum had always hated it. Dad's house was palest pink with red shutters at the windows and a red front door. Really pretty!

"Dad, did you *buy* it?" I said.

"No way!" Dad chuckled. "You know me… not the sort to get tied down! No, I just rent it. A bit of it. This bit!"

He led us down some steps, to a little dark door. The door opened on to an underground room. Dad lived in the basement!

"Basements are fun," said Dad. "You can look through the window and see people's legs."

"You can see their knickers!" cried the Afterthought.

"You can't," I said. "And if you could, you shouldn't look." I felt that *someone* had to control her; I owed it to Mum.

The Afterthought just scrunched up her face and went skipping away after Dad into the back room.

"This is where you two will sleep… you don't mind sharing a bed, do you?"

"Sharing with her? She snores!" shrieked the Afterthought.

"I do not," I said, angrily. And if me and the Afterthought were sleeping in the back, where was Dad going to sleep?

The basement only had two rooms, plus an outside loo. It didn't even have a proper kitchen; just a curtained-off corner with a sink and a stove. And no bath! What did we do when we wanted a bath?

Dad said he had an arrangement with the woman who owned the house. "Baths once a week! No problem."

"But where are you going to *sleep*?" I said.

"Don't you worry about me," said Dad. "I'll be OK on the sofa."

"Just stop fussing," said the Afterthought. "You sound like Mum!"

"Now, now!" said Dad. "Enough of that. How about we hit town?"

The Afterthought wanted to go and have the tea that Dad had promised us, so we walked down the hill to the town centre and there was the sea, all greeny-grey and heaving. The Afterthought immediately screamed that she wanted to go on the beach! She wanted to paddle! She wanted to collect shells! Dad said she couldn't just at the moment as the tide was coming in, fast.

"You could go on the pier, if you like."

"Yes!" cried the Afterthought. "Go on the pier!"

I said, "What about tea?" but she wasn't bothered about tea any more. The pier was far more exciting!

Actually, it was. The pier was brilliant! First off you came to a great cavern full of slot machines that you could gamble on. Dad went and changed some money and gave us a bag each of coins to play with. The Afterthought rushed shrieking from game to game, losing all her money (though she did win a bead necklace and a butterfly hair clip). I tried to be a bit more scientific about it, and study the form first. Studying the form is what Dad did with the gee-gees. He used to find out how many races the horses had run, and how many times they had been placed (come first, second or third). The way I did it with the slot machines, I stood watching people, seeing how much money they put in and what they got back – if anything. If it looked like a good bet, then I would have a go. Dad laughed and said I was following in his footsteps. I felt like I was at one of the

casinos in Las Vegas! I still didn't win anything, though, not even a butterfly hair clip, so I don't think I will follow in Dad's footsteps. It was quite fun, but I don't like losing money! I suppose I am a bit like Mum that way.

After the slot machines we walked on, along the pier, past rows of little shops selling souvenirs. I bought a stick of Brighton rock to send to Vix, and the Afterthought clamoured for a cuddly toy from a Hurlaball stall, so Dad said he'd have a shot and hurled three balls and won a white rabbit for her. We would both have liked to have tattoos done – "Semi-permanent. Guaranteed six weeks!" – but unfortunately the stall was closed. However, as Dad pointed out, we could always come back another day. We were there for the whole summer!

On our way to the end of the pier we passed a stall that was making doughnuts, and all stopped to have one. Dad said, "It's a hungry business, having fun!" While we were eating our doughnuts a most extraordinary bird came walking past. It was the size of a chicken, with huge webbed feet that plopped and plapped. I threw it a piece of doughnut, and the Afterthought cried, "Dad! Look! A goose!"

Dad said, "That's not a goose, you goose! It's a seagull."

I couldn't really say anything, since I had thought it was a goose, as well. I had no idea that seagulls were so huge!

"Eat up," said Dad. "There's more delights waiting for us."

We hurried on, through another casino – even more crowded and even noisier than the first one. Mum would have hated it! – and finally came out at the far end of the pier. This was where all the rides were. There were so many of them, all crammed into this one small space, that we hardly knew which to try first. The Afterthought wanted to go on the Crazy Mouse and the Waltzer. I fancied the Turbo Coaster, Dad fancied the Dodgems. There was also something called the Sizzler Twist, which was awesome!

"Oh, and look, look!" cried the Afterthought. "Dad, look! Bumper Boats! Oh, look! Helter Skelter!"

"*Belter Skelter*," I said, but the Afterthought was well hyped and didn't even hear me.

In the end we tried all of them, one after another. Dad shrieked with everybody else on the Sizzler Twist!

The Afterthought then caught sight of a
Funny Foto booth, where you stuck
your face into a hole and had your
photo taken as either a fat lady in

a skimpy
bathing
costume or a

skinny man in voluminous trunks.
She dragged Dad over there, while I
stood and watched. I didn't think I
wanted my photo taken as a fat lady!

While I was waiting, a couple of girls came strolling
past. They looked at Dad and the Afterthought's faces
peering through the holes and sniggered. I don't think
they realised that they belonged to my dad and my sister.
Dad then appeared from behind the skinny man figure,
and I could see these two girls sort of… giving him the
once-over. It was quite strange, watching girls not much
older than me eyeing my dad! As they went on their way
one of them said, "Cool!" and I couldn't help giggling.

"What was that all about?" said Dad.

By now I was giggling so much I could hardly speak.
I said, "D-Daddy drool!"

"*Daddy* drool?"

I had to explain it to him. Dad did laugh!

He said, "Where did you get that ridiculous
expression from?"

"From this magazine," I said. "One that Mum won't let me read any more."

"I'm not surprised," said Dad.

"She won't let us do *anything* any more," said the Afterthought. "She won't let me have my kitten!"

"Oh, for goodness' sake! Don't start," I said.

We were having such a great time! I didn't want the Afterthought going and ruining it by being mean about Mum.

Fortunately, Dad was already leading us back through the second lot of slot machines, where the music was so loud you could hardly hear yourself speak. *Definitely* not Mum's scene!

We retraced our steps, past the rock shop and the doughnuts and the semi-permanent tattoos, with the Afterthought clutching her rabbit and me clutching my stick of rock.

"Hang about!" said Dad. "This isn't fair… I must get something for Steph! What shall I get you? What would you like? How about a bit of Flower Power?"

Flower Power was a stall where you had to fire rubber suction darts at a big dartboard, which instead of being covered in numbers was covered in pictures. Top prize was a vanity case full of make-up. Wouldn't I have loved that! But I don't think darts was Dad's game as all he won was a flower. It was a very pretty flower, made of silk, with red petals and beautiful blue frondy bits, so I was quite pleased with it. I think I would have been pleased with anything that Dad had won! The man who owned the stall said it was a passion flower. Dad fixed it in my hair, and gave me a big kiss.

"That's what you are," he said. "My passion flower!"

I blushed like crazy, but I thought that I would keep my flower for ever. I said, "Thanks, Dad! It's gorgeous!"

Needless to say, the Afterthought wanted to be a flower, too, so Dad had another go, but this time all he won was a common or garden tulip, a vulgar yellow thing, all stiff and starchy. You can't very well wear a tulip in your hair! And you can't say to someone that they are your tulip. Not without it sounding totally ridiculous. I was so glad that I was a passion flower!

By now it was quite late and Dad decided we should go and eat. We left the pier and walked along the front, and it was so exciting because the lights were all twinkling, and everywhere you looked there were people enjoying themselves, and all around was the sound of music being played. Loudly, in some cases! I thought that Brighton was promising to be every bit as wild and wicked as I had hoped it would be.

We went into a restaurant and Dad asked us what we wanted to eat. The Afterthought immediately said, "Fish and chips!"

"*Sam*." I looked at her, reproachfully. "You know we don't eat animals any more!"

"Fish aren't animals," said the Afterthought.

"They are!" I said. "We had all this out with Mum!" We'd discussed it in great detail, only a few weeks ago. Mum had said that now she didn't have Dad to cater for, she was going to follow her conscience and become a veggie. She said that she wouldn't dictate to me and the Afterthought, we would have to follow *our* consciences, but she said she would like us to go away and think about it. So we both thought about it, and for once we'd been in total agreement with Mum. Eating animals was *cruel*. We had agreed that in future we weren't going to do it. And now here was the Afterthought prepared to go back on her word at the very first opportunity!

"Fish are *fish*," said the Afterthought.

"Yes, and they suffocate!" I said. "When they're taken out of the water they can't breathe. They flop, and gasp, and—"

"Just shut up!" screeched the Afterthought.

"But you *agreed*," I said. "You agreed that it was cruel!"

The Afterthought stuck out her lower lip, which is this thing she does when she's sulking. I turned to Dad.

"We talked about it," I said. "We had this long discussion! We said we were going to be veggies."

"Oh, stuff that!" said Dad. "Another of your Mum's crazy ideas."

"Dad," I said, "it's not crazy! Fish can *feel*. They *suffocate*."

"Everyone's looking at us," said the Afterthought.

"Not surprised," said Dad. "This does happen to be a seafood restaurant!"

I felt my cheeks grow red. I hate being the centre of attention! Unless, of course, it's for a good reason. I mean a *nice* reason. But this wasn't.

"Oh, now, come on, Passion Flower!" Dad blew me a kiss across the table. "What the eye doesn't see, the heart can't grieve over. Your mum won't know."

Yes, I thought; but that would be disloyal. I mean, we'd agreed!

"I'm going to have cod," said Dad. "What about you, Face Ache?"

The Afterthought giggled, and said that she would have cod, too.

"Passion Flower?"

I sighed. There really wasn't anything else on the menu. The only dish that wasn't fish was garlic mushrooms, which I can't stand. I suppose I could just have had chips and bread and butter. I thought afterwards that that was what I should have done, but instead I weakly gave in and ate fish, which I regret to say I greatly enjoyed, though I paid the price later, when we got home and I found a worried message from Mum on my moby. I had not only eaten poor suffocated fish, I had also forgotten to ring her, so now I had *two* things to feel guilty about. I called her back at once and said that I was sorry.

"There's just been so much going on!"

"Oh, I'm sure," said Mum.

"I'm sorry, Mum! Really! Do you want to speak to Dad?"

"Only if I must," said Mum.

I looked across at Dad. "Do you want to speak to Mum?"

"Do I have to?" said Dad.

Honestly! It's a real puzzle, sometimes, knowing what to do about parents. They can just make life *so* difficult!

# four

ON SUNDAY WE went down to the beach. Brighton beach is full of pebbles, so that you can't walk on it in bare feet but can only hobble and hop, going Ow! Ouch! Ooch! as you do so. Dad said that we had better buy some flip flops for ourselves. He said, "I'll pay for them. I'm quite flush at the moment." And then he winked and patted his pocket and said, "Money! What's it for, eh? If not for spending?" My feelings *exactly*! Dad and I do agree about quite a lot of things.

The Afterthought and I both had our swimming cozzies on under our clothes, but the water was too cold for swimming so in the end we just paddled. Quite childish, really! But Dad paddled with us, and when we'd had enough paddling he taught us how to skim stones across the surface of the waves. I discovered that I was quite good at it. Dad cried, "Way to go! That's my girl!" and I felt myself glowing. The Afterthought scowled, and threw as hard as she could, but all her stones just sank.

While we were there, the tide started going out, leaving a beach that looked quite grey and dismal. I looked hopefully for rock pools, but there didn't seem to be any; just endless pebbles and damp sand. I remembered once when we'd gone on holiday to Cornwall and found lots of baby crabs, the size of 5p pieces, and tiny little transparent prawns, all squiggling and squirming.

"Do you remember?" I said to the Afterthought. "We wanted to take some back for Mum to cook."

"They wouldn't have made much of a meal!" chuckled Dad.

"Anyway, it would have been a horrid thing to do," I said.

"No, it wouldn't!" yelled the Afterthought. "We could have had prawn cocktails!"

She had cheered up now that I wasn't beating her at stone skimming. She'd found some seaweed to pop, which seemed to amuse her, and had started making a collection of interesting shells which she said she was going to "do things with".

After a bit it clouded over. Dad said it looked like rain and we'd better decamp, so we put our shoes on and scrabbled back up the beach and sat snugly in a café on the front and watched as the rain lashed down. The Afterthought clamoured to go on the pier again, but Dad said we could do that tomorrow. He said he'd got a better idea for the afternoon.

"I thought we might go to Hastings and look at Battle Abbey."

Me and the Afterthought must have registered total moronic blankness, because Dad had to explain. "1066? Battle of Hastings? William the Conqueror?"

"Oh!" I said. "King Harold!" Importantly, to the Afterthought, I added, "He was the one that got an arrow through his eye."

Even the Afterthought had heard of King Harold. At least, I suppose she had. I had certainly heard of him when I was her age but I don't know what they're teaching ten year olds these days.

"Are we agreed?" said Dad. "Go to Hastings?"

"How do we get there?" I asked, as we squelched our way home through the rain.

"Drive! It's only just along the coast."

"You've got a *car*?" I said. He'd left our one for Mum to use. Mum had said – a bit sniffily, I'd thought – that from now on he would have to learn to rely on his legs. *If* he still knew how to put one foot in front of the other. "Which I doubt."

Dad was famous for going everywhere by car! Even just over the road to post a letter.

"There she is." Dad pointed, proudly, as we turned into his road. "Vintage motor, that is!"

I looked at it, dubiously. It was what I would have called an old banger, only I didn't say so as Dad was obviously pleased with it. But I didn't think Mum would be too happy at the thought of him taking us anywhere in it. It had great rust patches all over, and holes, and one of the bumpers was half-hanging off.

"Old Rover," said Dad. He patted it affectionately. "They don't make 'em like that any more!"

"Dad, it's *beautiful*," crooned the Afterthought. Honestly! There were times when she could be such a creep.

As we were going down the basement steps, a woman came out of the front door above us. At first all I could see were a pair of red strappy sandals which made me positively ooze with envy. They were the sort of sandals that I'd always desperately wanted to buy and which Mum would never let me.

"All that money for a few strips of leather? Totally impractical! Wouldn't last five minutes."

Above the sandals were legs that seemed to go on for ever – and ever – and ever. Like *really long*! They finally disappeared into a mini skirt. Well, more of a micro skirt, really. Mum would have had a fit if I'd gone out in a skirt like that! The woman who was wearing it was actually too old, I would have said, to be showing all her legs (not to mention half her bum). I mean, she was about Mum's age, but just quite *incredibly* cool, with this long honey blonde hair and gorgeous golden tan. Dead cool!

She called out to Dad, "Hi, Daniel!" Even her voice was sexy. Very low and husky, like her throat was full of gravel. Or maybe she just smoked. Dad said, "Hi, Shell! Girls, this is my landlady, Shelley Devine. Shell, these are my two girls… this is Passion Flower, this is my little Afterthought."

I said hallo and shook hands, in a proper grown-up manner, but the Afterthought turned shy and hid behind Dad. She is so weird! Ms Devine got into a little red sports car that was parked next to Dad's old banger. As she drove off, Dad thumped on the roof and Ms Levine stuck her hand out of the window and gave a wave.

"That's quite a woman!" said Dad.

"I bet if *she* walked past the window we'd be able to see *her* knickers," said the Afterthought. "If she wears any," she added.

Honestly! I was shocked. I mean, this child was *ten years old.* I would never have dreamt of saying a thing like that at ten years old! I think Dad was a bit shocked, too; or at any rate, somewhat taken aback. He said, "All right, Face Ache! That will be quite enough of that."

"Some people don't, you know," hissed the Afterthought, as Dad opened the front door. "Wear any knickers, I mean."

"Look, just button it!" I said. Mum wouldn't have let her talk like that, and I didn't think I should, either. "Don't be so disgusting!"

"I'm not being," said the Afterthought. "I just—"

"Well, don't! Shut up, or I'll tell Dad."

She pulled a face at that, but at least it kept her quiet.

After we'd changed our clothes and dried ourselves off we piled into the banger. I let the Afterthought sit in front with Dad, as it meant so much to her, but then I got worried because there wasn't any seat belt. Mum would never forgive me if we had a crash and the Afterthought went through the windscreen. I said, "Dad, it's against the law!"

"Not in this car," said Dad, cheerfully. "This car was built in the days before seat belts."

It didn't stop me worrying. The Afterthought could still go through the windscreen.

Fortunately she didn't. We got there unscathed! Dad didn't even have to swear at anyone, which is what Mum complained he usually did.

Battle Abbey was really quite interesting, as old monuments go. I am not really an old monument sort of person, I am more into modern stuff, but I thought it would be a good thing to tell our history teacher about when I went back to school. She hadn't been best pleased with me last term. She had told me that I obviously had "no feel for the historical perspective", whatever that was supposed to be. It's possible she was referring to the fact that my last three pieces of homework had come back marked C-, but that was because it was all

boring stuff about wars and politics. I am not into wars and politics. I am into *people*. Like I once read somewhere that James I used to go to the toilet just anywhere he felt like going. Behind pillars, behind curtains, in the middle of the floor if no one was watching. Truly gross! But that is the kind of thing I find interesting.

I suppose poor old Harold being shot in the eye is quite interesting, although somewhat bloody.

After we'd done the Abbey, and I'd bought some more postcards, we got back into the banger and banged our way back to Brighton. We didn't eat out that night but bought pizzas and took them home with us. I chose a Margherita. Cheese and tomato: *no meat*. Dad and the Afterthought both had ones covered all over with bits of dead flesh. Ham and salami and pepperoni. I was cross with the Afterthought, because this time there wasn't any excuse, and I lectured her about it all the time we were eating. The Afterthought said I was a nag. She said, "Dad! Tell her to stop. I can eat whatever I like!"

"She can, you know," said Dad.

I said, "But Dad, we gave Mum our word! It's a matter of principle. Mum feels really strongly about it."

Dad pulled a henpecked face and said, "Tell me something I don't know! I lived with it for nearly seventeen years. The thing is, Honeybun, your mum may be an admirable woman – she *is* an admirable woman! –

but she gets these bees in her bonnet. If she wants to live on nut loaves and lettuce leaves, that's up to her. But she's got no right to impose it on you."

I pointed out, in fairness to Mum, that she wasn't imposing, that me and the Afterthought had decided for ourselves; but the Afterthought, guzzling pizza as fast as she could go, and spraying disgusting gobbets of food all about the table, screamed that she had changed her mind.

"I can change my mind if I want! Can't I, Dad? I can change my mind!"

"You most certainly can," said Dad.

"*See?*" The Afterthought stuck out her scummy pizza-covered tongue and gave me this look of evil triumph. "You can't tell me what to do!"

I decided that from now on I would simply wash my hands of her.

"I'm going to go and write my postcards," I said. I'd got one for Vix, one for Mum, and one for Gran, Mum's mum, who is very old and lives in a home. "Is it OK if I give Vix your email address?" I said to Dad.

Dad said, "Sorry, kiddo! I don't have one any more. Got rid of the computer. It had to go."

The Afterthought cried, "*Dad!*"

"Needs must," said Dad. "When a man is cruelly turned out of his home without a penny to his name, he has to raise money as best he can. It's no big deal! Who needs possessions, anyway?"

I thought, I do! I like possessions. I love all my ornaments and my trinkets and what Mum calls my bits and pieces. Not to mention *clothes*. I would have wardrobes full, if I could! I said this to Dad, but he just laughed and told me that it was nothing but useless clutter.

"You think it's important, but it isn't. What's important is being able to throw everything you own into a couple of carrier bags. That way, you can be ready to get up and go at a moment's notice. Clutter just holds you back."

Dad certainly didn't have any clutter. He'd taken almost nothing with him when he left home, and he didn't seem to have bought anything since. I couldn't live like that! I don't want to get up and go at a moment's notice. I like to take stay put. I suppose I am not very adventurous.

I wrote my postcard to Vix:

Brighton is wicked! Yesterday I gambled on the slot machines, but didn't win anything, but Dad won a passion flower for me. It is very beautiful. Haven't met any boys yet!!! Will look for some tomorrow.
xxx Steph.

Then I wrote to Gran, printing it in my best handwriting as her eyesight is not too good:

DEAR GRAN, WE ARE STAYING WITH DAD IN BRIGHTON. IT IS VERY NICE HERE. YESTERDAY THE WEATHER WAS GOOD BUT TODAY IT IS WET. WE HAVE BEEN TO SEE WHERE THEY FOUGHT THE BATTLE OF HASTINGS. IT WAS VERY INTERESTING. LOVE FROM STEPHANIE.

Lastly I wrote to Mum:

Dear Mum, I am sorry I forgot to ring you. I would ring you in Spain if I knew the number. I cannot email you even if I had your email address as Dad has had to sell his computer. Today we went to Hastings to see where Harold was shot in the eye. It was very educational. Lots of love from Stephanie.

In spite of my resolve to wash my hands of the Afterthought, I still got stuck with her next day as Dad said he had things to do.

"Like work, you know? Keep the wolf from the door."

I was a bit surprised by this, as I was not used to Dad working, though of course he had on occasion. I asked him whether it was in an office, which seemed to amuse him.

"Me? In an office? That'll be the day!"

"So what sort of work is it?" I said. I wasn't being nosy, I just wanted to be able to tell Mum: Dad's got a proper job! But I don't think it was a proper job; not exactly. Well, not a being-there-every-day-from-nine-till-five sort of job. Dad just said that he had "this nice little number going", and he winked as he said it, which made me think perhaps I'd better not ask any more questions. Just in case. Not that I thought it would be anything *illegal,* but maybe something it would be better for us not to know about, like – well! I couldn't actually think of anything. At least Dad was earning money; that was all that mattered. (I decided, though, that I wouldn't mention it to Mum. Not unless she asked.)

I was really pleased that Dad had found himself a job. What I wasn't so pleased about was the prospect of having to cart the Afterthought round with me wherever I went. I'd been kind of hoping that she might go off somewhere with Dad and leave me to my own devices.

How could I look for boys with a whiny ten year old clinging to me?

"Wouldn't you rather go with Dad?" I said.

But Dad didn't think that was such a good idea, and neither did the Afterthought.

"I want to go on the pier!" she said.

So off we trolled to the pier, with our pockets full of money. (I'd given Mum's cheque to Dad, to put in the bank, and he'd said to go to him whenever we needed anything.)

"I don't think we ought to gamble again," I said. I braced myself for a load of bad mouth along the lines of "I can do what I like! You can't order me about!" but to my surprise the Afterthought agreed. She said, "No, 'cos when you gamble you lose all your money."

I was so knocked out that I asked her what she *did* want to do. She said she wanted to get a printed T-shirt and be tattooed. I said, "Right! Let's do it."

I got a blue T-shirt with *PASSION FLOWER* printed on it. The Afterthought got a red one with *My dad's mad and bad*. She said it was something she'd read somewhere and she thought it was funny. I suppose it was, quite.

"Let's put them on!" she said, so we both dived into the Ladies and did a quick change. After that we went to the tattoo place, which was now open, and got ourselves tattooed. I asked for a passion flower to be put on my

arm, but the woman who did the tattoos couldn't find a picture one so she did a different sort of flower, red, like I wanted. I wasn't quite sure what it was, but it was pretty and I was pleased with it. The Afterthought was *sickening*. She got a heart with the words *I love my dad*. Truly disgusting and yucky! I didn't say so, however, as we were getting along really well and I didn't want to ruin things.

I asked her what she would like to do next. I could have thought of a zillion things that *I* would have liked to do, such as going round the shops, but I didn't mind humouring her, just so long as she behaved herself. "Do you want to stay on the pier or go somewhere else?"

The Afterthought said she wanted to stay on the pier. "I want something to eat! I'm starving."

I was quite hungry myself. Dad didn't really have very much to offer in the way of food; all we'd had for breakfast was a plate of soggy cereal and a piece of shrivelled toast. The Afterthought said there was "a dear little café" near where we had come in, so we turned and started walking back towards it. I held my arm out in front of me, admiring my tattoo. I giggled.

"Just as well they wear off… Mum would have a fit!"

"Don't see why," said the Afterthought. "It's not like a *real* tattoo… I wish I could have a real tattoo! I bet Dad would let me."

I thought that Dad just might. "Don't you dare ask him!" I said.

"Why not?"

"'Cos Mum wouldn't like it."

"Mum wouldn't see it!"

"She could hardly miss it," I said. "Unless you had it done somewhere stupid, like your bottom."

"I'd have it done *here*." The Afterthought tapped the side of her nose. "I'd start a new fashion… I'd have a nose tattoo! And she still wouldn't see it, 'cos we're not going to go back. So there!"

I stopped. "What do you mean, we're not going back?"

"We're not going back!"

I said, "Of course we're going back. Don't be silly! We're only here for the holidays."

"That's what you think," said the Afterthought.

I said, "That's what I *know*."

"Well, you know wrong! She doesn't want us back. Dad said. She told him he could have us, and welcome. So that's it! We're staying with Dad."

"That is such rubbish," I said. How could we stay with Dad? It was great being with him for a short time, but Dad couldn't look after us. He didn't have the room!

He didn't have a kitchen, he didn't have a bathroom, he didn't have anywhere to keep food. We couldn't stay with Dad! Trust the Afterthought to get it wrong.

"Mum just meant *for the summer*," I said. "He was welcome to us *for the summer*. While she had a break, 'cos we'd been mean to her."

"We weren't mean to her!" shrilled the Afterthought. "She was mean to us! She was mean to *Dad*. Throwing him out like that!"

There was no denying that Mum had been quite hard on Dad.

"You're always on her side," grumbled the Afterthought.

"Oh, shut up!" I said. We'd been getting on *so* well. I'd almost been quite fond of her, just for a few minutes. Why did she always have to go and ruin everything?

We found the dear little café and sat at a table outside, eating doughnuts and drinking milk shakes. Probably fattening, but who cared? We were on holiday!

While we were sitting there, I noticed this boy that kept glancing at me from the doorway of a slot machine place. He was with two other boys, but they were busy at a machine, pulling levers and pressing buttons. The one who kept glancing at me seemed more interested in – well, in *me*! I edged my chair round ever so slightly so that he would get a better view of my profile. I don't mean to boast, but I am quite proud of my profile. You know how with some people, movie stars, for instance, they can look fab full face? But then they turn their heads and you suddenly see that they have pointy noses or double chins and look quite ordinary. Even, in some cases, plain. A great disappointment! Especially if you have been thinking to yourself that this is my dream guy and then you see their nose all beaky or their chin sagging down like a waterlogged sock. I mean, talk about *disillusion*.

I have studied myself long and hard in Mum's dressing table mirror, which is one of those with wings on either side, and I feel reasonably confident that my profile would live up to expectations. Assuming, that is, that you had looked at me full face and liked what you saw. I am not being vain here! I think it is important to know these things about yourself; it can save a lot of heartache.

It can also save a lot of heartache if you don't have beastly ten-year-old brats dragging round with you, clocking everything with their beady little eyes and shrieking out their vulgar comments.

"Why do you keep staring at that boy?" demanded the Afterthought, in these loud clanging tones that everybody within a ten-mile radius could probably have heard.

I said, "Which boy? I'm not staring."

"Yes, you are! You're *ogling*."

What kind of word is that for a ten year old to use?

"I suppose you fancy him," she said.

I tossed my head. "You can suppose what you like."

Usually when I toss my head, my hair goes swirling round. But I'd forgotten – I'd tied it in bunches. Reluctantly, I decided that it would look a bit too obvious if I pulled it loose. A pity! My hair is black, like Dad's, and quite thick. Vix once said it was sexy!!! I suppose that really *is* boasting, though I'm only repeating what she said.

"Do you think he's good-looking?" said the Afterthought.

I did, as a matter of fact, but I wasn't giving her the satisfaction of knowing.

"Do you?" I said.

"No," said the Afterthought. "He's got silly hair! He's *ugly*."

I felt like bashing her. He wasn't ugly! And his hair wasn't silly, he'd had it dyed blond and gelled it so it was all gorgeously stiff and spiky. The Afterthought just had no sense of style at all.

"Looks like a hedgehog," she said. "Oh, gobbets! He's coming over... he's going to talk to you! *Yuck!*" She hung her head over the side of the table and pretended – noisily – to throw up.

"Why don't you go back home?" I said.

"Don't want to go back home," said the Afterthought.

"Well, then! Go and buy yourself a funny hat, or jump off the end of the pier, or something."

"No." She settled herself back on her chair. "I want to stay here and see what happens."

Spiky Hair was making his way towards us. The Afterthought was right. He was going to talk!

"Hi," he said.

I said, "Hi," and blushed furiously into my milk shake.

"Love the T-shirt! Is that your name? Passion Flower?"

"No, her name's *Stephanie*," said the Afterthought. "Who're you?"

Spiky Hair grinned. "I'm Zed. Who are you?"

"I'm Samantha and I'm staying," said the Afterthought.

"Quite right," said Zed. "Who knows what I might get up to?"

The Afterthought made a hrrumphing noise and twizzled her straw in her milk shake.

"She your chaperone?" said Zed.

"No," I said, "she's my sister and I'm stuck with her."

"Know the feeling," said Zed. "I've got one at home. A right pain."

"You can say that again," I said.

The Afterthought made another hrrumphing noise.

"Elephants run in the family?" said Zed.

Hah! That got her. She hates being made fun of. Crossly, she shoved her chair back.

"I'm going to feed the seagulls. Don't be all day!"

Zed promptly sat himself down next to me. "Why not?" he said. "In a hurry?"

I shook my head.

"Here on holiday?"

"We're here for the whole of the summer," I said. I didn't want him to think we were just, like, day trippers. "We're staying with our dad." And then I got brave and said, "How about you?"

"Me? I'm a denizen! I live here."

"You *live* here?"

"People do. You'd be surprised!"

"I wouldn't," I said, "'cos my dad does." But I did think Zed was lucky!

"So where d'you live, then?"

I pulled a face. "Nottingham."

"With your mum?"

"Yes. They're separated."

"Mine, too. We have something in common!" He grinned at me. I grinned back. "We both live with our mums, and we both have little bratty sisters... d'you ever manage to get out without her?"

I said, "At home, I do. At home we have practically nothing whatsoever to do with each other. It's difficult, here."

"How about in the evening?"

"Oh! Well – yes." Was he asking me out??? "I guess in the evening she could stay with Dad." I couldn't be expected to keep an eye on her *all* the time.

"There's a gang of us meet up in the Bluebell Caff. Just a bit further along from the pier." He pointed. "Feel like coming along? Eight o'clock?"

I nodded, breathlessly. Zed said, "Great. See you there!"

It was at that moment that my little bratty sister came wandering back. She watched jealously as Zed returned to his mates.

"See you where?" she said.

I said, "None of your business. I have a date!"

And I bought another postcard, to send to Vix.

Have met a Gorgeous Guy! We're seeing each other tonight. Will tell more later! xxx Steph.

# five

"I SUPPOSE I have to ask where you're going," said Dad.
"And what time you're going to be back... that's what
your mum would do, isn't it?"

"She's going on a date," said the Afterthought. "With
a *hedgehog*!"

"Really? That's novel," said Dad. "Where does one
hang out, with a hedgehog?"

Glaring at the stupid Afterthought, who vulgarly
stuck her tongue out, I told Dad that we were "just
meeting up in a café."

"OK," said Dad. "You know the rules. Home by...
what shall we say? Ten? Does that sound about right?"

"Mum wouldn't let her stay out that late," said the Afterthought.

"She would, too!" I said.

"Not with a boy you don't even know," said the Afterthought.

"So how do I *get* to know him?" I said. "If I'm not allowed to go out with him?"

"Good question," said Dad. "How old is he?"

I thought probably he had to be sixteen. Even, maybe, seventeen. But it seemed safer to say, "About my age?"

"More like *twenty*," said the Afterthought.

"Dad, he isn't!" I cried.

"OK, OK," said Dad. "I believe you. Just behave yourself – and make sure you've got your phone with you. There!" He sat back, beaming. "I reckon that's my parental duty taken care of."

The Afterthought sucked in her breath and slowly shook her head, like some cranky old woman. I really couldn't understand what her problem was; I'd have thought she'd be pleased to be left on her own with Dad. She just didn't like me having fun was what it was. She'd been behaving like the worst kind of spoilt brat ever since Mum and Dad split up. Mum said she was insecure and we must make allowances, and I did try, but what about *me?* I was insecure, too!

"I bet he does drugs," said the Afterthought.

"He doesn't!" I shrieked.

"Bet he does!"

If the Afterthought had said something like that in front of Mum, Mum would have gone half demented. It would have been, like, full-scale panic and Stephanie-I-don't-want-you-going-out-with-that-boy! Dad – dear old Dad! – just snapped open another can of lager and said, "Why do you bet? What do you know about it?"

"She doesn't know anything!" I said. "She's all mouth!"

"Well, just watch it," said Dad. "Just don't do anything I wouldn't."

I sent the Afterthought a look of triumph and shot out of the door before she could think of any other objections to raise. Nasty little troll! I was just glad Dad didn't take her seriously. Not that anyone could, though that wouldn't have stopped Mum. But Mum wasn't here. I was *free*!

I rushed off, down to the seafront. Only my second day in Brighton, and already I'd got myself a date! Vix would be *soooo* envious.

I was wearing my new passion flower T-shirt and my denim shorts with the flip flops Dad had bought me. I didn't think I would need a jacket as it was really hot and anyway I didn't want to spoil my outfit. I guess what I really mean is, I didn't want to cover up my tattoo!

Zed was already there, in the café, waiting for me. I was quite relieved to see him as you are always a bit

worried – well, I am always a bit worried – that maybe
people won't turn up. That is, *boys*, when they ask you
out. This happened once to Vix, and it really upset her. It
took her ages to get her confidence back.

Zed waved when he saw me. "Hi, Passion Flower!" It
killed me, the way he called me that. So much more
romantic than Stephanie!

The others who were with him all turned to look.
There were two boys, that Zed introduced as Chaz and
Nick, and two girls, Paige and Frankie. Paige and
Frankie were truly cool. They both looked like top
fashion models and about eighteen years old, though it
turned out they were only just starting Year 12 so they
couldn't have been. They were still older than me, but I
hoped perhaps they wouldn't realise as I do look quite
mature for my age. At least, that is what I have been told.
It is horrid if everyone knows how young you are as they
immediately start treating you like a child, and it makes
you feel really inferior. I discovered that all five of them
lived in Brighton and went to the same posh school, the

Academy. That was the way they referred to it, just "the Academy", like everyone would automatically know what it was, like Eton or Harrow or somewhere. I knew it had to be posh as they all spoke in these voices like the Queen. What Dad calls "fraffly". Paige asked me what my accent was. I didn't even know I had an accent! Paige said that she collected them – accents, that is. Zed told me that she was going to be an actress and needed to be able to speak in different kinds of voices.

"Like wotcha, cock! Cor blimey, mite!"

I think he was pretending to be Cockney. Paige shrieked, "Zed, don't! That is ex*cru*ciating!"

All five of them then started putting on different accents and shrieking loudly at the tops of their voices. They didn't seem to mind that people were looking at them.

"So what *is* yours?" said Paige, when they had simmered down.

"It isn't anything," I said. "It's just ordinary."

They found that really funny. Paige shrieked, "Just ordinary!" and they all fell about.

"It's Sherwood Forest, isn't it, Passion?" Zed put his arm round my shoulders and hugged me to him. "'Er do come from Robin 'ood territory, don't 'ee, lass?"

"Oh, Zed! Muzzle it!" said Paige.

Chaz told me not to worry. "You don't really sound like that. It's just Zed and his cloth ears."

"This is the guy," said Nick, "who thought Chopin's

Funeral March was the Wedding March… tum-tum-ti-*tum*, tum-ti-tum-ti-tum-ti-tum."

Everyone screeched, and so I screeched, too, though to be honest I didn't really know whether the tum-ti-tums were supposed to be the funeral thingie or the wedding thingie.

I was beginning to feel a bit out of my depth and was quite glad when Zed decided that it was time to move on.

"Let's take Passion on the pier! Show her the attractions."

Me and Zed led the way – with Zed holding my hand. I couldn't wait to write and tell Vix! – and the others ambling along behind. As far as I could make out, Chaz and Paige were an item, and Nick and Frankie. I wondered if I might be going to become an item with Zed… I'd never been an item with anyone before. Not properly. I'd once gone out with a boy in my class, Jimmy

Hedges, for almost a term, but the whole time I'd been going with him I'd been sighing over another boy, Chris Whitwood, who was in Year 10. I'd thought Chris was the dog's dinner. Now he just seemed like… rubbish!

Being on the pier with Zed was utterly, totally different from being on the pier with the Afterthought. Even from being on the pier with Dad, though we did lots of the same things. We screamed on the Sizzler Twist and clutched each other on the Turbo Coaster and giggled on the Crazy Mouse (which was really for little kids). We also went on the Dodgems, where the boys had a great time deliberately bumping into each other. The man in charge grew really angry and threatened to switch off the power if they didn't stop it. As we got out, he shook his fist and yelled, "You poxy kids!"

I said, "What is he so cross about?"

Zed explained that he didn't like us bashing up his cars.

I said, "But I thought that was the whole point of it?"

"Yeah, I guess that's why they're called Dodgems," said Frankie.

I blushed; I'd never thought of the name as having any sort of meaning. I could see that it was stupid of me, but there wasn't any need for her to use that sarcastic tone of voice. I had the feeling Frankie didn't like me very much, though I couldn't imagine why. I thought maybe she secretly fancied Zed, and was jealous of me.

She gave me this *filthy* look when I started shivering, and Zed took off his jacket and put it round me. She really didn't like that!

"You wouldn't be much good on the nudie beach," said Zed. "You'd have goose pimples all over!"

"W-what n-nudie beach?" I said.

"Ours, of course! Don't you know about it? We're famous for our nudie beach! People come from miles, just to see the sights."

"Yeah, and what sights!" said Nick.

He and Zed then began to act out all the sights that could be seen on the nudist beach. Paige and Frankie joined in, and within minutes they were all doubled over, screaming with laughter. I was laughing, too, but was

91

more embarrassed than anything. I could feel myself starting to grow gently warm and pink. Please, no! I thought. But once you start, you just can't stop. The more I tried to fight it, the worse it became, until warm turned to hot and pink turned to red and before I knew it I was lit up like a beacon. Like a big human blood orange. Being embarrassed by s.e.x. is *so* belittling! So horribly *young*.

"Oh, poor Passion!" cried Frankie. "We've made her blush!"

"That's because she's a nice girl," said Zed. "Unlike some of us."

"Speak for yourself," said Frankie.

PASSION

"You're just a tart," said Zed. "C'm 'ere, Passion! Let me give you a hug… I *like* nice girls!"

"Drop dead," said Frankie. And then she smiled sweetly at me and said, "I suppose you don't have nudists in Nottingham?"

I wished I could have thought of some smart remark, but of course I couldn't. I never can. Vix can! I just go all dumb and stupid.

"You lot naff off," said Zed. "Me and Passion want some quiet time."

The others drifted away, and Zed and I were left on our own. I thought he might try what Mum would call "funny stuff", and I was sort of a bit apprehensive, not knowing whether I could handle it, and a bit tingly, half hoping that he would, but in fact he didn't, he just walked me back home (though still keeping his arm round me). He said that he was going to be in Switzerland for the whole of the next four weeks, staying with his dad, and when he told me that my heart went *thunk*, because I thought it meant I would never see him again, but he said that he wanted to, and he took my phone number so that he could call me as soon as he got back. I couldn't help wondering whether he was just saying it, or if he really would. (I also wondered how I was going to survive for a whole month without him.)

"You don't think I mean it, do you?" he said. Help! He'd read my thoughts! "You think it's something I say to all the girls. But it's not! I really, really want to see you again."

He said it like he truly meant it. He really did want to see me again! I knew that Vix would warn me not to get excited. Not to count on it. She still hadn't properly got her confidence back after her bad experience. Boys weren't to be trusted! They'd tell you one thing, then do another. I knew all that. I knew that I wasn't cool like Paige and Frankie, that I didn't go to a posh school or have rich parents. I knew that Zed could quite easily meet up with some gorgeous girl on the plane on the way back from Switzerland and forget all about me. I knew, I knew! But I could dream, couldn't I?

It was gone half-past ten when I got back indoors. Dad didn't say a word! I don't think he even noticed. I mean, he noticed that I was back, but I don't think he realised what the time was. Or maybe he did, and he simply wasn't bothered. Mum would have been practically foaming at the mouth!

The Afterthought, thank goodness, was asleep, and I slid into bed really *sloooowly* so as not to wake her, but at breakfast next morning she started up.

"You didn't get in at ten o'clock! I know, 'cos I stayed awake!"

I said, "If you'd had a periscope and shoved it out the window you'd have seen that I was standing right outside."

"Doing what?" said the Afterthought.

I said, "None of your business!"

"Smooching, I bet! With the Hedgehog. I told Mum you'd gone out with a hedgehog."

"You told *Mum*?"

"When she rang."

"When did she ring?"

"Last night, after you'd gone."

"Checking to make sure I wasn't letting you starve," said Dad. "OK, girls!" He pushed back his chair. "I'm off. Got things to do. I'll see you later. Be good!"

"What shall *we* do?" said the Afterthought, as the door closed behind Dad.

I felt like saying, "You do what you want, I'll do what I want," but I knew that I couldn't. I'd promised Mum I'd look after her.

"What would you like to do?" I said.

"Go on the beach and find shells!"

"Wouldn't you rather do something more adventurous?"

"Like what?"

"I don't know! Like... go and see the nudist beach?"

"I don't want to see a nudist beach. I want to find shells!"

"The nudist beach would be more fun."

"I'm not taking my *clothes* off!" roared the Afterthought.

"I don't mean take your clothes off, I mean look at the other people with *their* clothes off."

"No! I don't want to. I want to find shells!"

I gave in. "Oh, all right," I said. Zed wasn't around, so we might just as well go and find her stupid shells as anything else. "I must buy another postcard for Vix."

"Why?" The Afterthought looked at me, slyly. "I s'ppose you're going to boast about the Hedgehog!"

I wondered to myself if I had been that tiresome when I was ten years old. I didn't think you had to be; I mean, just because you were ten years old. I knew some ten year olds who were actually quite nice. Vix's little brother, for instance. He was really cute! I thought, "Trust me to get lumbered with a bratty one." I was still trying to come up with some kind of crushing retort when there was a knock at the door and when I went to open it Ms Devine, Dad's landlady, was standing there.

"Hallo!" she said. "Stephanie, isn't it? Is your dad in?"

I said, "No, he's just left. He's gone to work."

"Work?" said Ms Devine. She sounded surprised, as if she didn't expect Dad to work. That made me think that she must know Dad quite well.

"He's got this little number," I said.

"Really? Well! I wonder if you could give him a message for me? Just whisper the word *rent* in his ear. Could you do that?"

"Rent," I said.

"He'll understand," said Ms Devine. "Just tell him… Shell said, rent."

We watched as Ms Devine's legs went back up the basement steps.

"She didn't sound cross," I said.

"Why should she sound cross?" said the Afterthought.

I wasn't sure; it was just that I was used to people sounding cross with Dad. I gave him the message when he got back that afternoon. Dad said, "Oh, yes! Don't worry about it. I have it in hand. What say we go up the road for a Chinese?"

"What, now?" I said.

"Why not now?" said Dad.

I said, "It's only five o'clock!"

"So what?" said Dad. "There's no law says you can't eat at five o'clock, is there? I don't know about you, but I eat when I'm hungry!"

It was one of the *best* things about being with Dad: there wasn't any routine. There weren't any set rules. We had meals at all odd times, just whenever Dad decided we should. Sometimes we had takeaways, sometimes we went out and sometimes we made do with stuff out of a tin. We got up when we liked, and watched telly when we liked, and went to bed when we liked. We never knew when Dad was going to be home or when he was going to be out. When he was home we all did things together, like maybe we'd mosey into town (Dad's way of putting it!) or jump in the car and go for a drive.

One day we went to see the Royal Pavilion, near the seafront. The Royal Pavilion is very historical, being built for George IV. It is full of many beautiful and precious objects. From the outside it looks like white onions shining in the sun. Well, I thought it looked like white onions. The Afterthought said it was more like meringues, and promptly decided that she had to eat meringues *immediately*, so we all rushed madly around in search of a tea shop, ending up in this big hotel on the seafront, feeling very grand.

This was the sort of thing that happened when you were with Dad. One day it would be spaghetti hoops out of a tin, the next it would be meringues, with tea in china tea cups, in a posh hotel. You just never knew.

When Dad wasn't home we were left to our own devices and could do pretty well whatever we liked. No one to fuss and bother over us! No one to huff and puff when we forgot to phone, or didn't arrive back when we were supposed to. Mum would have had fifty fits, but Mum wasn't there, she was living it up in Spain. She'd sent us a postcard saying, *Dear Both, I am having a wonderful time, I hope you are. Be good! Love, Mum.* Nothing about missing us, or looking forward to having us back. None of her little mumsy frets about whether we were eating properly, whether the Afterthought was behaving herself, whether I was keeping an eye on her. She was just busy enjoying herself. So after that I stopped feeling guilty when the Afterthought stayed up till the small hours and Dad let her watch unsuitable programmes on the telly and we both stuffed ourselves with junk food day after day. We could do what we liked!

The only thing I didn't like was having to lug the Afterthought with me wherever I went. Occasionally, as we searched for shells, or played the slot machines, or wandered along the seafront nibbling candy floss or eating ice creams, I'd catch sight of Zed's friends, either all four of them together or in ones and twos. They'd wave at me and say hallo, but they never asked me to join them. I felt sure this was because I had my little bratty sister with me. I asked her one day if she wouldn't rather I left her at home.

"What for?" she said, instantly suspicious.

"Well! I don't know… wouldn't you like to do things with your shells? Or watch telly, or something?"

"You just want to get rid of me," she said. "But you can't, 'cos you promised Mum! You told her you'd look after me."

"I'm trying to," I said. "That's why I thought maybe you'd rather stay at home. I don't want you to wear yourself out," I said.

The Afterthought said she wasn't wearing herself out, she liked going on the pier, and going on the beach, and paddling in the sea.

"Anyway," she said, "I'm not allowed to stay home by myself. You know Mum wouldn't let me."

Since when had that ever bothered her?

"Let's go and look round the shops," she said. "Let's buy things!"

"We can't," I said, "we haven't any money." I'd asked Dad for some, but he'd forgotten to go to the bank and until he did we only had enough for the odd ice cream or bottle of Coke.

"We can still go and *look*," said the Afterthought.

As we were wandering round the shops, we bumped into Paige, and another girl. One I hadn't seen before. Paige was quite friendly. She said, "Hi, Passion Flower!" It was the only name she knew me by. I would have liked it to stay that way, but my dear little sister immediately had to go and pipe up.

"Her name's not Passion Flower, it's Stephanie!"

Paige could obviously see me squirming, and took pity on me. She said, "If I were called Stephanie, *I'd* change it to Passion Flower. This is Marie-Claire, by the way. She's our exchange. *Elle ne parle pas beaucoup d'anglais*, do you?" Marie-Claire giggled and shook her head. "*Et moi*," said Paige, "*ne parle pas hardly any français du tout*. I suppose you don't, do you, Passion?"

"Only *un peu*," I said. "*Un très peu.*"

"Anything would be a help," said Paige. "Frankie speaks it OK, but she's not here. She's gone off to the Algarve for a fortnight. The boys are away, as well, so I'm all on my ownsome. I'm taking Marie-Claire to see the Pavilion. Feel like joining us?"

I was all ready to leap at the chance when *she* had to go and pipe up again. "We've already been to the Pavilion!"

"Yes, and you thought it was boring, so you might just as well *shove off*," I said, "and do something else!" I gave her a push. "We don't need you hanging around whining."

I know it was rather harsh of me, and that I wasn't making allowances, but she was *such* a nuisance.

"I'm going with Paige," I said. "You go and do your own thing."

"You can't go!" shrilled the Afterthought. "It costs money to get into the Pavilion! You haven't got any!"

"I have," said Paige.

"So naff off," I said; and I gave the Afterthought another push. A bit harder, this time. "Go on! Hop it!" And then I remembered, and tossed the front door key at her. "Go home and do your shells! I'll see you later."

"Will she be OK?" said Paige.

"She knows where we live," I said. I had had just about enough of my whiny little sister. Mum was off enjoying herself and obviously couldn't care less, so why should I?

I stayed out most of the day. After we'd been to the Pavilion we went on a little train that ran along the seafront, which was quite fun – though it would have been more fun if Zed had been there! But then everything would have been more fun if Zed had been there. Feeling rather bold, I said, "What about the nudist beach?"

"*Boring,*" said Paige. She turned to Marie-Claire. "You don't want to voir people sans clothes, do you?"

Marie-Claire giggled and said, "Sans clothes? Ah, mais non!"

"Me neither," said Paige. "Let's go back home and get something to eat. Come on, Passion! You, too."

Paige lived in a house a bit like the one that belonged to Ms Devine. It was all furnished with beautiful delicate antiques – little spindly chairs that looked as if they would collapse if you were gross enough to sit on them, and sofas covered in wonderful satiny stuff, and tiny little round tables standing on one leg.

Paige seemed to take it all for granted. She led us down some indoor stairs to the basement, which was about the same size as Dad's but had been turned into one big room with a counter running down the middle. On one side of the counter was a kitchen that Mum would have died for. It was the sort of kitchen you see in glossy magazines at the dentist's, with rows of shiny pots and pans, and strings of garlic hanging from the ceiling, and this vast great stove with double ovens. I tried not to let my mouth hang open, as I didn't want to look like a yokel, but I was distinctly gob-smacked. I asked Paige if Zed lived in a house like hers, and she laughed and said, "Zed! His place makes this look like a cupboard." So then I was even more gob-smacked and wondered what he saw in me and whether he really would ring me when he got back.

It was half-past four when I arrived home. I banged at the door, and Dad let me in.

"Where's your sister?" he said.

I said, "Isn't she here?" and my heart did this great walloping *thump* almost into my throat.

"She's not here," said Dad. "I thought she was with you?"

"She was," I said, "but I – I sent her back."

 Dad looked grave. It takes a *lot* to make Dad look grave. "When was this?" he said.

"I don't know! About... eleven o'clock?"

"For heaven's sake, Stephanie! That's over five hours ago. Where can she have got to?"

# six

DAD WENT RUSHING up the basement steps and out into the street, as if perhaps the Afterthought might have been following without me noticing. I raced after him.

"You're telling me," said Dad, "you haven't seen her since *this morning*?"

"I s-sent her back home," I stammered. "I g-gave her the key!"

"Not good enough," said Dad. "Not good enough! Totally irresponsible! Where's she likely to be? Think! Where do you usually go?"

I said, "The p-pier?" It was the only place I could think of. The Afterthought loved the pier. She was pier-crazy. She'd told me only the other day she would like to live on it, in a little booth like the one where the woman did the tattoos.

"We'd better go and look for her," said Dad. "Come on! Both of us! Two pairs of eyes are better than one."

We jumped into the car and roared off towards the seafront. Dad told me again that I had behaved totally irresponsibly. I felt like saying that so had he and Mum, what with Mum running off to Spain and leaving us with someone who couldn't even look after a pot plant. I mean, she *knew* what Dad was like, it wasn't fair expecting me to cope all by myself. Dad didn't have any right to heap all the blame on me! The only reason I didn't say it was that I was too worried about the Afterthought.

We reached the pier, and Dad dropped me off.

"You go and see if you can find her in there, I'll drive along the front. I'll meet you back here."

It wasn't easy, searching for the Afterthought on a crowded pier, but I did my best. I searched *all* through the slot machine rooms, both of them, squirming and burrowing amongst the bodies. I checked all the rides, I checked the tattoo booth and the cafés, I even went into the Ladies and called out, "Samanth*aa*?" but she wasn't anywhere to be found and I was getting really scared.

Dad was waiting for me in the car. I went tearing over, hoping and praying that I would see the

Afterthought beaming up at me, or even scowling up at me, I wouldn't have minded! But Dad was on his own.

"No luck?" he said. "Are you sure you looked all over?"

"Dad, I looked *everywhere*," I said. "She's not there!"

"OK, hop in. We'd better drive round a bit. Keep your eyes peeled."

We drove slowly round the streets, me with my head hanging out of the window. A couple of times I saw girls that looked a bit like the Afterthought, and my heart leapt, but as soon as we got close I could see that it wasn't her.

"I just don't know what possessed you," said Dad. "Leaving a ten year old on her own!"

"I told her to go back home," I wailed.

"Stephanie, she's *ten years old*. What were you thinking of?"

What I'd been thinking of was me. Having some time to myself, for a change, without the Afterthought tagging on and ruining things.

"I can't cart her round with me everywhere I go!" I said.

"Well, I can't be expected to take her with me," said Dad. "I've got work to do. Are you keeping your eyes open?"

Resentfully I snapped, "*Yes*!"

I hung my head back out of the window. Already I was beginning to have scary pictures of the Afterthought on the evening news, and to hear the voice of the announcer saying how police were gravely concerned for the safety of a ten-year-old schoolgirl, Samantha Rose, who had disappeared while staying with her father and sister in Brighton. The Afterthought had been told repeatedly, we had *both* been told repeatedly, never to talk to strangers, never to get into a car with anyone we didn't know. Not even if it was anyone we did know, unless we knew them really well. We had had it drummed into us by Mum. Every time we went anywhere, it was, "Just remember, d—"

"*Don't talk to strangers!*" We'd chant it in unison. "*Don't get into cars!*" It had become like a sort of joke. "Mum!" we'd go. "Stop fussing!"

I knew that the Afterthought wouldn't normally do anything silly. I mean, she wasn't daft. But if she'd been in one of her moods, there was no telling what she might get up to. I imagined her marching down to the pier, angry and defiant, thinking to herself that if I was having fun, she was going to have fun, too. I imagined someone watching her, seeing that she was on her own. Offering to buy her an ice cream, or take her on the turbo coaster, and the Afterthought, thinking she would show me, going off with them, all innocent and trusting, and—

"Stephanie?" said Dad.

"W-what?" I smeared the back of my hand across my eyes.

"You OK?" said Dad.

No! I wasn't OK! My little sister had gone missing and it was all my fault.

"We'll just do one final check at home," said Dad, "see if she's turned up, then we—"

He stopped, as the car began to judder and ground to a halt.

"What is it?" I said. "What's the matter?"

Dad banged his fist down, hard, on the steering wheel.

"We're out of gas, is what's the matter!"

"Oh, Dad!" I said.

"Don't you *Oh Dad* me! I didn't know we were going to have to drive halfway round town looking for your sister. Well, that's it! No car."

"There was a petrol station just a little way back," I said. "We could—"

"Could what?" said Dad. "Fill her up? What with? Air?"

I bit my lip.

"I didn't bring any money," said Dad. "Unless you've got any?"

But I hadn't; not enough for petrol. Not even enough to just get us back home.

"W-what shall we d-do?" I said.

"Walk," said Dad. "Come on! Shake a leg."

Dad set off really fast, with me trotting beside him.

"If she's not th-there," I said, "do we g-go to the police?"

Dad frowned. "We'll keep our options open."

"But, *Dad*—"

"I said we'd keep our options open."

"But, D—"

"Stephanie! Just remember, you're the one who's caused all this."

I was starting to cry again. "M-maybe we should r-ring Mum," I said. "She'd know what to do!"

"Your mother's the last person we want to bring in," said Dad. "Oh, now, come on, Passion Flower!" He slowed up, to put an arm round me. "You've got to have a bit more backbone than this. She'll show! She's probably pottering about on the beach. We didn't look on the beach, did we?"

Through sniffles, I said, "The t-tide was in."

"Well. OK! So—" Dad waved a hand. Even he was starting to sound a bit uncertain.

"Dad, we've got to go to the police!" I said.

"All right, all right! We'll go to the police. Let's get home first."

You will never believe it! We had just arrived back, and gone down the basement steps, when my dear little sister comes skipping out of nowhere, her face one big beam from ear to ear, going, "Dad, Dad! A lady up the road has got some kittens. She said I could have one! Oh, Dad, *can* I? Please, Dad, say I can! *Please!*"

All my instant relief turned to absolute fury. "Where have you been?" I shrieked.

"Up the road! To see the kittens! Dad, they are so *sweet*."

"There you are," said Dad. "I told you, didn't I? All that fuss! I said she'd show up."

"But where have you *been*?" I screamed it at her, really loud. "I told you to come home!"

"I did," she said. "But then I got bored, so I went for a walk, and I met this lady, and she was getting out of her car and she dropped her shopping and all these tins of cat food went rolling about, so I helped her pick them up and she said she'd got this cat that had had kittens and would I like to see them? So I said yes, and I went in with her and—"

"You went indoors? With a total stranger? Are you *mad*?" I said. "She might have kidnapped you!"

"What would she want to do that for?" said the Afterthought. "She's got kittens! There are two black ones and a ginger one and the *dearest* little fluffy one, and she said if I wanted one I could have one, like, *now*, immediately, 'cos they're ready to leave their mum, so please, Dad, *can* I? Please?"

"Don't let her!" I said. "She doesn't deserve one!"

"I do! Don't be horrible!"

"You don't," I said, "and I'm not being. You deserve to be smacked. We've been looking all over for you!"

"And there I was, just up the road," said the Afterthought, as if that made it all right. "Were you worried about me?"

"Yes, we were!" I snapped. "Though goodness knows why."

"You shouldn't have left me on my own," said the Afterthought. "You're supposed to be looking after me. Anything could have happened! I could have got lost, I could have got run over, I could have been *abducted*."

"I wish you had!" I snarled.

"Girls, girls!" Dad held up a hand. "Don't let's fall out. All's well that ends well. I'll tell you what… let's go and fill up the jam jar then drive out somewhere for a meal."

"I thought you didn't have any money?" I said.

"Money? I've got loads of money! I've got a whole wad." Dad winked. "Close your eyes, both of you."

Obediently, we closed them. I heard Dad's footsteps moving across the room.

"OK! You can look…
*now*!"

We looked. I think my mouth fell open. Dad had a whole fistful of notes!

"See? I told you I'd been working!"

"It looks like you've won the lottery," squealed the Afterthought.

"I wish!" said Dad. "But I'm not complaining. So come on, let's go!"

All the way back to the car, the Afterthought kept on about her kittens. Dad said that we would discuss it over dinner.

"One tiny little kitten," said the Afterthought, as she and I sat in the car while Dad set off for the petrol station with the spare can from the boot. Empty, needless to say. I couldn't help thinking that if it had been Mum, the spare can would have had petrol in it. But if it had been Mum, we'd probably never have needed to use the spare can in the first place.

"He's all little and tiny," crooned the Afterthought.

"Kittens usually are," I said.

112

"Yes, but he's like a little mini one."

"In that case," I said, "there's probably something wrong with him."

"There isn't! Don't be so horrid!"

"Well, but look, what's the point?" I said. "You know Mum won't let you keep it."

"I told you, we're not going back to Mum!"

It worried me when she said that. I knew it was nonsense, but it still worried me.

Dad drove us all the way to Lewes, where he said there was a nice little pub. We sat outside, in the garden, and the Afterthought ate scampi and chips, which made my mouth water, only I wasn't sure whether scampi counted as animal so to be on the safe side I had a baked potato filled with coleslaw, which in truth was rather boring. But sometimes you have to make sacrifices, for the good of your soul. I just wished Mum could have been there, to see me. *And* to see the Afterthought.

She was still carrying on about her kitten. In the end – of course! – Dad said she could have it. The Afterthought was always able to get round Dad. Mum once said, "If that child asked you for an elephant, you'd go out and buy her one."

I'm not sure he'd have bought an elephant for me, but then I would never have asked.

When he said she could have her kitten, the Afterthought flew round the table and hugged him.

"Darling Dad! Sweet Dad!"

Yuck yuck *yuck*. But Dad seemed to like it. He promised that we would ring the cat lady as soon as we got home. The Afterthought flashed me this look of triumph.

"Mum will never let her keep it," I said. I knew this wouldn't make an atom of difference, but I just wanted to hear what Dad had to say.

Dad didn't say anything: the Afterthought got in first.

"It's nothing to do with Mum! Mum won't know anything about it!"

"She will if you try taking it home."

"We're not going home! Are we, Dad? We're not going home! We're staying with you."

"Would you rather stay with me?" said Dad.

"*Yes!* 'Cos you give me kittens!"

"Stephie? How about you?"

"I – don't know," I said. "How would we live? And what about school?"

"Who cares about school?" scoffed the Afterthought.

"I do!" I said. "I've got friends."

"Only Vix!"

"She's my *best* friend. I've got others!"

"Mum doesn't want us back, anyway," said the Afterthought.

"Dad!" I appealed to him. "That's not true, is it? It's not true! Tell her!"

"There, there." Dad patted my hand. "Don't get in a lather. It may never happen."

I said, "What? What may never happen?"

"Anything," said Dad. "The end of the world, little green men from Mars… just take life as it comes. That's my motto."

"Mum still won't let her keep the kitten," I said.

"Stephanie, you worry too much," said Dad. "It ain't worth it. It'll all come out in the wash."

There were times when I really couldn't understand what Dad was talking about. It was one of the things that used to get Mum so mad at him. She called it "evading the issue".

"Can't give a straight answer to a straight question!"

The minute we got home, the Afterthought insisted that Dad rang about the kitten.

"Don't forget, it's the fluffy one… I want the fluffy one!"

She got the fluffy one.

I have to say, he was really cute! Like a little black furry imp, skittering about the place. The Afterthought couldn't think what to call him, so Dad suggested Titch.

"Yes," crowed the Afterthought, "'cos he's titchy!"

I said, "What happens if he grows big? He might grow enormous!"

"In that case," said Dad, "it will be funny… *Titchy, Titchy, Titchy*! And then this monstrous great bruiser of a cat lumbers up."

"He's not going to be a bruiser," said the Afterthought. "He's going to stay as a titch!"

Having a kitten really transformed the Afterthought. I suddenly realised, it was months since I'd seen her happy and laughing. Ever since Dad left home, she'd been just about as mean as she could be. She'd been really hateful to Mum. Looking back I could see that I hadn't behaved all that well, but the Afterthought had deliberately gone out of her way to be hurtful. I could understand why Mum had packed us off. I would have packed us off. But now she had Titch, the Afterthought was all smiles. She told me that I could share him.

"He'll be my cat, but you can cuddle him. If you want to."

Anyone would have wanted to! He was just so adorable. I didn't say any more about Mum not letting us keep him; I thought that even Mum, once she saw him, would be unable to resist. I still couldn't really believe what the Afterthought had said, about us not going back, but I did ask Dad if I could telephone Mum and find out when she was expecting us.

"Best not," said Dad. "She gave me strict instructions… *only call if there's an emergency*."

"But you have got a number for her?" I said.

"I've got a number," said Dad. "But it would be as much as my life's worth to let you use it! You know how your mum terrifies me."

"Oh, Dad!" I said. "She doesn't!"

"Are you kidding?" said Dad. "She could even frazzle me down a phone line!"

He was making like it was a big joke, but he wouldn't let me have the number. He said Mum really had told him that she didn't want to be disturbed.

"But how are we to know if she's all right?" I wailed.

"She'll be all right," said Dad. "Don't you worry about your mum. She's one tough cookie!"

A few days later, we had a postcard from her.

Dear Girls. sun, sand and sangria! Total bliss. Why didn't I do it before??? Hope your dad's coping. Hope you're having fun. Lots of love, Mum

I pored over it, reading and re-reading it. Mum was happy. Yeah! She was enjoying herself. Good! She sent her love. *Lots* of love. That meant she wasn't mad at us any more. But she still didn't say she was missing us, or was looking forward to having us back. It really was a bit worrying.

As well as a card from Mum, I had one from Vix, who had gone on a camping holiday to France with her mum and her little brother.

Hi, Steph! We just arrived last night so I haven't had time to check out the boy situation. I will report! Has Zed come back yet? Has he rung you? I hope you won't be too upset if he doesn't, you know what boys are like. But if he does you must be cool! Whatever you do, don't show him that you are pleased or he will think you are too easy. Anyway, that is my advice.
xxxx Vix

It was now almost a month since Zed had gone to Switzerland. I'd been counting the days, secretly marking them off on the wall of the toilet, down low where it couldn't be seen. I did it like people in prison do, if they are in solitary confinement:

1/ 2/ 3/ 4/ 5/

I couldn't tick them off on the calendar, or the Afterthought would have noticed. I didn't want her making any of her silly remarks.

I knew the exact day when Zed would be back. I spent the whole of it in a state of jitters, waiting for him to ring. He didn't! I thought perhaps he was suffering from jet lag (from Switzerland?) or that he hadn't arrived home until late. He would ring tomorrow! Maybe. Or maybe not. I couldn't help drooping, just a little. I knew that Vix was bitter, on account of her bad experience, but a month is a terribly long time! I didn't really think, probably, that Zed would remember me. I mean, there wasn't any reason why he should, it is not as if I am anything special. I know I am quite prettyish and look mature for my age, but a boy like Zed could get any girl he wanted. He could get rich girls, cool girls, girls who really were sixteen. Not just pretending!

These were the things I told myself, to stop from being disappointed. If I had bumped into Paige or any of the others I might even have been brave enough to ask them, "Is Zed back yet?" But I hadn't seen any of them since the day the Afterthought gave us such a fright. We hadn't really been out all that much, which was partly because it had been raining rather a lot, and partly because we didn't have any money. Dad had peeled some notes off his wad and given them to us, but we had spent all that and now Dad said he was "a bit skint" until something else turned up. In other words, he didn't have any money, either! I couldn't help wondering what had happened to all the rest of the wad, but I didn't like to

119

ask in case he thought I was nagging. (Which was what he used to accuse Mum of doing.)

Now that she had her kitten, the Afterthought didn't mind staying in. Sometimes Dad was home, but most often it was just me and the Afterthought by ourselves. When we weren't playing with Titch, I helped the Afterthought do things with her shells. She was sorting them into different shapes and sizes, and then painting them with nail polish in all different colours. I'm not sure what she was doing it for, but it kept her happy. I didn't really mind. At least we were friends again.

It was the day after Zed was due back, when we were in the middle of shell painting, when my mobile rang. It rang and rang, and I couldn't find it! I was racing round the room in total panic, trying to trace the sound, when the Afterthought calmly picked up a cushion, and there it was. I shrieked, "Gimme, gimme!" but she danced away, out of reach, behind the 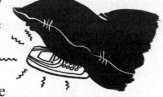 sofa. In this very posh voice she said, "This is the Rose residence. How may I help you?" And then she pulled a face and said, "It's W."

I said, "What?"

"W," said the Afterthought. "P. Q. *Zed*. The alphabet person. Your beloved... it's all right! I've pressed the secrecy button, he can't hear."

I snatched the phone from her and dashed into the bedroom. *Cool.* I had to be *cool.*

"Hi," I drawled, doing my best to sound like Paige and Frankie.

Zed said, "Hi, Passion!" Was he *laughing*? I went hot all over. Don't say that stupid child hadn't pressed the secrecy button after all! "Have you missed me?"

I knew Vix would tell me to say no, but I'd gone and said yes before I could stop myself. Zed said, "Good! I wanted you to. Hey, listen! There's a party on Saturday. Feel like coming?"

Vix would have been so cross with me! I forgot all about cool. I even think I might have *gushed.* Yuck! I can't stand people who gush. But being invited to a party by this totally gorgeous male! I couldn't wait to write a postcard…

Before I could do that, however, I had to ask Dad whether it was OK for me to go. I knew if it had been Mum the answer would have been a big firm NO. She would have reminded me that I was only fourteen – *just* fourteen. She would have pointed out that I didn't really know Zed properly. She would have said that in any case he was too old for me. (She only liked me to go out with boys my own age. Anything over fifteen and she freaked.) Mum would also have wanted to know where the party was at, and if I'd said "Haywards Heath" that would have been it. The final nail in the coffin. *No way!*

When I said Haywards Heath to Dad he just said, "Oh, that's all right! Twenty minutes on the train. No problem."

I almost jumped in the air and clapped my hands. Three cheers for Dad! Dad *trusted* me. That was the difference between him and Mum: Mum treated me like a child.

"Don't you want to know what time she's going to be back?" said the Afterthought. She didn't say it to be mean; more like she was actually trying to be helpful. Trying to remind Dad of his responsibilities.

Dad said, "Yes! Absolutely right. What time are you going to be back?"

I hesitated.

"What time would your mother say?"

Mum wouldn't have let me go in the first place; but if she *had* let me go, she'd have told me to be back at some absurd sort of hour, like half-past nine.

"How about midnight?" said Dad. "That sound about right? For a party?"

The Afterthought looked at me, wide-eyed. I gulped and said, "Y-yes! Midnight sounds fine."

I couldn't believe it! *Midnight.* I flew at Dad and kissed him.

"That is just so brilliant!" I said.

Dad looked pleased. "You're welcome. Just have a good time.

I intended to!

# seven

I COULDN'T THINK what to wear for the party. It was obviously important. Very important! Not to say, *crucial*, if I wanted Zed to stay interested in me. But I'd only brought a few clothes with me, and now I didn't have any money to buy more. I tried asking Dad, but he shook his head, regretfully, and said, "Sorry, kiddo! Funds are a bit short right now."

For several minutes I felt quite cross and resentful, wondering what had happened to the cheque that Mum had given us. I knew what had happened! Dad had gone and spent it. He had spent *our money*, just as he had spent Mum's.

But then I remembered how he had taken us on the pier that first day, and given us change for the machines, and how he had bought us our flip flops and paid for our tattoos and our T-shirts; and all the times he had taken us out to dinner, and the trips to Lewes and to Hastings, and the Afterthought's kitten; and I reminded myself, also, that if it had been *Mum* who was in charge of us, I wouldn't be going to the party anyway. So then I stopped being resentful and decided to make the best of things.

The Afterthought helped me. Now that she had Titch, and was happy again, she was really eager to make up and be friends. We laid out all my clothes on the bed, trying to decide which were most suitable for a party. The Afterthought picked up my one and only dress, bright pink, with a halter top. Greatly loved by Mum! I was quite fond of it, too.

"You think I should wear that?" I said.

"It's what makes you look prettiest," said the Afterthought. "But it also makes you look *young*."

"Forget it!" I waved the dress back on to the bed. No way did I want to look young! "What about that?" I pointed to a top that I particularly liked as I thought it flattered me. "Could I wear that?"

"Mm…" The Afterthought studied it, through half-closed eyes. "That would be OK."

"What shall I wear with it? Shorts?" No! Zed had already seen me in my shorts. "These!" A pair of Capris

– well, that's what the girl in the shop said they were. Trousers that came to just below the knee. I'd seen Frankie wearing some a bit like them, so I knew they were OK. Frankie's had been flowery. Mine were white, like the top, with red embroidery and red fringes. I held them up against me and gave a little twirl. "What do you think?"

"Shorts are best for showing off your legs," said the Afterthought. "But trousers are more sophisticated."

I settled for the trousers, with my flip-flops since my only sandals were too infantile for words, and as the Afterthought said, "You can't wear trainers. Not if you're going to be dancing." She then had a brilliant idea for what she called "an assessory". (I didn't tell her that the word was *accessory*. It didn't seem fair, when she was trying so hard to help.) She suggested that I should use some of her bottles of nail polish to paint my nails all different colours.

"Would that look good?" I said, doubtfully.

The Afterthought said it would be the height of fashion, she had seen it in a magazine, so I took her at her word and gave myself two nails blood red, one green, one gold, and a silver thumb!

"See? I told you!" said the Afterthought. "That looks fab. And look, look!" She snatched up my silk flower, the one Dad had won on the pier, and thrust it at me. "You could put this in your hair!"

126

It was strange, the Afterthought had absolutely *no* sense of style when it came to herself, but she could choose stuff for me OK.

"What are you going to wear on top?" she said. "Your denim jacket?"

It was all I had, and it was quite old and tatty, but the Afterthought said that denim was meant to be old and tatty. She said, "It would look really sad if it was new. Like you'd gone out and bought it specially."

Oh, wise Afterthought! I hugged her and said, "From now on, you will always be my fashion consultant."

I was meeting Zed and the others in the Bluebell Café, so Dad said he and the Afterthought would give me a lift down to the front.

"It's all right," he said, "I won't get out of the car and shame you. I'm sure you wouldn't want to be seen with a tatty old dad! Incidentally, you're looking very chic, if I may say so."

I was glad Dad thought I looked chic. I just hoped Zed did, too!

He was there in the café, with Paige and the other three. He was even more gorgeous than I remembered him! His hair was still blond, but now he had a deep golden tan to go with it.

"Yo, Passion!" He reached out a hand to pull me down beside him. I did so want to be cool and elegant! Instead, to my shame, I went and tripped over the leg of someone's chair and practically fell on top of him. Everybody thought it highly amusing, except for me. I, of course, turned bright red like a pillar box.

"Somebody's eager!" cried Nick.

"Somebody happens to have *missed* me," said Zed. "Isn't that right, Passion?"

"Don't be so big-headed!" Paige aimed a smack at him with a menu. "Boys!" she said. "Think they're God's gift!"

"We are," said Zed. "What would you do without us?"

"Get on very nicely, thank you," said Paige.

I felt that it was time to make a contribution, other than tripping over chair legs. Brightly I said, "What time does the party start?"

"Any time," said Frankie. "Just whenever we care to turn up."

"We'll be leaving in a few minutes," said Nick.

"Why, anyway?" said Frankie. "Do you have to go to bed early?"

She really *didn't* like me. But Zed did! That was all that mattered.

"So whose party is it?" I said, determined not to be squashed.

"Yes! Whose party is it?" said Zed.

"I don't know," said Chaz. "I thought you knew?"

"I don't know," said Zed.

"Well, somebody must! Whose party is it?"

In bored tones, Frankie said, "It's a friend of Gary Meldrum."

"Who's Gary Meldrum?" said Zed.

"I dunno," said Chaz. "I thought you knew?"

"I don't know!" said Zed.

"Oh, shut up!" said Paige. "You know perfectly well who he is. He was in Year 12. Don't take any notice of them, Passion. They are quite *stupid*."

When we walked up to the station, Zed held my hand all the way. Paige and Chaz held hands, too, but I noticed that Nick and Frankie didn't. That just made me think all over again that Frankie secretly fancied Zed and was jealous of me. I knew she was jealous of me because she actually tried to get rid of me! As we reached the station, she suddenly said, "Are you sure you're old enough to come to this party?"

"Of course she's old enough!" said Zed. "What kind of question is that?"

"She doesn't look old enough to me," said Frankie.

Zed said, "How old are you, Passion?"

I was so glad I hadn't worn the pink dress! Boldly I said, "I'm sixteen. Just," I added. I thought it made it sound more like the truth if I said "just", though I could tell from the way Frankie tossed her head that she didn't believe me. Zed did. He told Frankie to stop behaving like a mother hen.

"Come on, Pash! I'll get your ticket."

I suppose, really, what with equality of the sexes and all that, I should have said that I would get my own, but I didn't because I knew that Zed probably had loads more money than I did, and if I'd had to buy my own ticket it would have left me with about 2p in my purse. Which is always a bit scary.

We got to the party at eight o'clock, but we only stayed for an hour because Zed and Chaz decided it was boring and wanted to move on. I didn't find it boring! I thought it was fun. But it seemed there wasn't enough happening. Zed said, "This is not where it's at."

"So where shall we go?" said Frankie.

Chaz said he knew of something in Croydon. "We could try that."

"Let's do it!" said Zed.

I was a bit alarmed as I didn't know where Croydon was, but Zed assured me it was only a short train journey.

"Are you certain that you want to come?" said Frankie.

Zed said, "Of course she wants to come!"

"You mean, *you* want her to come."

"It's not a question of what I want," said Zed.

Paige said, "Oh, no? Since when?"

"We ought to put her on the train back," said Frankie.

Honestly! The cheek of it. Like it was up to her to decide my life for me.

"I'm coming," I said. "I want to go to a party!"

Frankie didn't say any more; just shrugged her shoulders. I felt triumphant. I had won! Zed paid for my ticket again and we all got on a train for Croydon. The journey was longer than the one from Brighton to Haywards Heath had been, so that it was nearly ten o'clock when we arrived. I thought, "I'll never be home by midnight!" but it was too late, now, to start worrying. It would have been altogether too babyish to have gone home.

I never did find out whose party it was. I'm not sure any of the others knew, either, except perhaps Chaz, who was the one who had suggested it. It was held in someone's flat, on the ground floor of a big old house, and by the time we turned up it had really got going. Lots of noise, lots of people, and music loud enough to blow your brain. Just the sort of party I would normally have loved! But right from the word go I had this feeling I had made a mistake. Frankie was right: I shouldn't have come! For starters, everybody was heaps older than I was. There wasn't a single person there who looked to be under eighteen. Most of them looked like they were in their twenties. It was difficult to find anything to drink that wasn't alcoholic, and I just knew that people were smoking stuff they shouldn't, and that some were doing worse than just smoking. I am not a prude! I am a very broad-minded sort of person. I believe that everybody should be allowed to do their own thing. But I didn't feel I was ready for this!

I didn't think that Zed was ready for it, either, in spite of being seventeen and going to a posh school. He started drinking almost immediately and just didn't stop, and although he wasn't drunk, exactly – at least, not falling-over sort of drunk – he became really silly so that I couldn't get any sense out of him. I asked him when we were going to go home, and he said, "Who knows? Today, tomorrow? This time next week? Maybe never!"

"It's getting really late," I said. "It's nearly half-past eleven."

Zed said, "Shock horror! Half-past eleven… soon 'twill be the witching hour! Ghoulies and ghosties and long-leggety beasties, and things that go bump in the night! Have a drinkie. Make you feel better."

He held out his glass, but I pushed it away.

"I think we ought to go," I said.

"Don't want to go," said Zed. "Having fun. Drink up and don't be such a misery!"

This time he actually tried to force the glass between my lips, and when I shoved it away it spilt all down his

133

front. Zed said, "Look what you've done! What a waste of good booze. Now I shall have to go and get some more."

He went weaving off, across the room. I didn't know whether to go after him or not. I didn't know what to do! I was starting to feel quite frightened. How was I ever going to get home? I looked round for the others, but they didn't seem to be there. Icy bullets went zapping down my spine. Suppose they had already left? I would be on my own with Zed! And Zed had gone silly, with too much drink. He wasn't going to take me home. Why had I ever come???

I'd come because I'd resented being pushed around by Frankie. Because I didn't want Zed thinking I was just a little kid. And now I was frightened and wished I wasn't here!

I suddenly became aware that someone was looming over me. A tall skinny man with a straggly beard. I'd already noticed him across the room, looking at me.

"Hallo!" he said. "What are you doing here?"

I felt sure there ought to be some witty kind of response to this question, but I couldn't think of one. I couldn't think of *any* kind of response. I was just, like, frozen.

"All on your own?" said Skinny. He leant over, and the beard waggled at me. I hate beards! "Been abandoned?"

I shook my head, very frenziedly, to and fro.

"No?" Skinny studied me, and waggled his beard again. He seemed friendly enough, but you can't trust men with beards. I knew this, because Vix had told me so. She had read it somewhere. (They grow beards to *hide* things.) "You looked a bit lost," he said, "that's all. I take it you belong to someone? Are you here with your mum and dad?"

Heavens! He thought I was a child. He was checking whether I would be missed if he made off with me. I gasped, "No, I'm – with my boyfriend. He's—" I flapped a hand in the direction in which I had seen Zed disappearing. "He's over there! I've got to… get him!"

I shot off across the room. I expect it probably sounds quite pathetic, but I was really scared. I wasn't scared that the skinny beard man was actually going to make off with me, because if he tried it I would scream the place down. *Someone* would notice. Wouldn't they? They couldn't all be drunk! I mean, some of them had to stay sober so they could drive home.

If they were going home. If it wasn't the sort of party where they all crashed out and didn't come to until the following day. I think that's what I was really scared of. Having to spend the night with all these druggy people! I was sure most of them were on something. Ecstasy or something. Zed could be, for all I knew. Boys from posh schools were always being busted for drugs. He was probably zonked out of his skull right now. If only Frankie hadn't been so unpleasant! If she'd just taken me to one side and said, "Look, Passion, you can't fool me! I know you're only fourteen. You really don't want to come to this party." Well, I might just have listened. Instead, she'd sneered and jeered and tried to make me feel stupid. It was her fault!

I knew it wasn't, really. But I was just so frightened! I was thinking of all the movies I'd seen (movies that Mum hadn't wanted me to watch but Dad had always let me) where innocent young girls had drugs pumped into  them and became helpless addicts living on the street, or died hideous contorted deaths, rolling their eyes and frothing at the mouth.

I blundered through a press of bodies and into the hall. I'd got to get away! I'd got to get back home! Someone grabbed me by the arm and I let out a yell.

"Passion?" It was Chaz. Chaz and the others! "Where's Zed? We're leaving."

The minute he said that, my heart stopped hammering, the bullets stopped pounding. Great waves of relief washed over me. I said, apologetically, that I wasn't sure where Zed was.

"I think he went to find some more booze."

"Oh, God!" said Chaz. Paige rolled her eyes.

"You stay here," said Nick. "We'll go and find him."

"Well, just hurry!" said Frankie. "We don't want to miss the last train."

Nervously, I said, "W-when *is* the last train?"

"Twenty-five after midnight," said Frankie. "Way past your bedtime," she added.

Paige said, "Shut up, Frankie!"

"Well, she shouldn't have come. *I'm* not taking responsibility for her. It's up to Zed."

"Zed couldn't take responsibility for a paper bag," said Paige.

Like Dad, I thought. Zed was just a younger version of Dad! He was doing to me what Dad had done to Mum. All of their married lives Dad had behaved irresponsibly; Mum had never been able to rely on him. He'd spent money they didn't have, he'd made promises he didn't keep, he'd just always, always let her down. The same as Zed had done to me!

I wondered miserably if it were true, what Vix had once

told me (something she'd read in a magazine) that girls often fell for boys who reminded them of their dads. It certainly seemed to be what I'd done. Well! I'd learnt my lesson. Next time I would make sure I chose someone solid and boring and responsible. I didn't want this happening again! Chaz and Nick came back, dragging Zed with them. Zed cried, "Hi! There's Passion!" and launched himself in my direction but fell headlong before he could reach me. Nick grabbed him just in time. "Passion, Passion!" cried Zed. "Where have you been all this time?"

It was quite embarrassing. I don't think I will ever take up drink.

We got to the station just two minutes before the train was due. It didn't get in to Brighton until gone one o'clock! I'd never in my life been out so late all by myself. Without Mum or Dad, that is. Paige said, "Don't you think you ought to ring someone and tell them you're on your way?"

I tried ringing Dad, but there wasn't any reply. I knew what had happened: Dad hadn't re-charged his mobile. He'd got a new battery for it, but he didn't always remember that it needed re-charging.

"No one there?" said Paige, sounding surprised.

I explained about Dad forgetting to re-charge.

"Don't you have a land line?" said Frankie.

I thought she said *landmine*. Bewildered, I said, "What's a landmine?"

138

Zed chortled. "Something you tread on and it blows you to smithereens!"

No one took any notice of him. Frankie, speaking very slowly and deliberately, as if I were half-witted, said, "*Land LINE*."

"An ordinary phone," said Paige.

"Oh! No, we don't have one of those," I said.

So then they all looked at me like I was some kind of alien. All except Zed, who was still sniggering to himself.

Suddenly, more than anything else on earth, I wanted to be home. *Really* home. Back in Nottingham, with Mum! I didn't care if Nottingham was dull and boring. I didn't care if Mum fretted and fussed and treated me like a child. I wanted to be treated like a child! I wanted to be fussed over! I would have given anything to hear Mum laying down her rules and regulations. *Don't talk to strangers. Don't get into cars... don't go off to wild parties with boys you don't know!*

I had thought I was so grown up. I had tried so hard to be cool and mature. All I'd succeeded in doing was frightening myself.

I felt ashamed, afterwards. When I looked back on it I felt that I'd behaved like a stupid baby. After all, what had happened? Nothing! No one had tried to abduct me, or have their way with me, or force me into taking drugs. There was a girl in my class at school, Rhiannon

O'Donnell, who went to parties like that all the time. Or so she claimed. Maybe she did. She'd started going with boys when she was only eleven. I hadn't gone out with a boy till I was thirteen! I decided, sadly, that in spite of *looking* mature I was obviously extremely young for my age. Vix, too! Because when I told her about the party she said that she couldn't have handled it, either. She said it was nice that we could admit these things to each other.

"Instead of just boasting, you know?"

I wished Vix could have been there with me, on the train that night. I wouldn't have felt so alone and so insecure. I knew that I was a nuisance, and that the others felt responsible for me. Not Zed, who was the one who had brought me. Zed was well out of it. But Paige and the two boys. Paige said they couldn't let me go home on my own, and Chaz and Nick agreed. Frankie just pulled a face. I knew what *she* was thinking... *I told you so*! I was grateful to Paige as I would have been really nervous of walking home by myself.

It was gone quarter-past one when I arrived back. I thought for sure Dad would be worried about me. Even Dad! I imagined him trying to ring me and discovering that his mobile wasn't charged. I braced myself for angry cries of "Stephanie! What time of night do you call this?" Instead, I found Dad slumped on the sofa, fast asleep, with the telly still blasting away. I wondered whether to simply turn it off and creep past into the

bedroom, but before I could do so Dad suddenly opened his eyes and said, "Steph? That you? I must have drifted off!" Then he sat up and stretched and said, "Had a good evening?"

I don't think he even noticed what time it was.

# eight

"HEY! STEPHANIE!" THE Afterthought shot up the bed and pummelled me into wakefulness. I opened a reluctant eye.

"Wozza time?"

"Nearly seven o'clock!"

"Too early! Go back to sleep."

"I can't, I'm awake!"

"Well, I'm not. Leave me alone!" I punched, irritably, at the pillow. "I didn't get to bed till half-past one."

"I know. I tried waiting up for you, but I fell asleep – and that was after *midnight*!" The Afterthought bounced, and my head went bang, thud, wallop. "I want to hear about the party! Tell me about the party! Was it good?"

I grunted.

"What did you do? Did you dance? Did the Alphabet person kiss you? Did you enjoy it?"

I said, "Yes, it was fun." And then I, too, catapulted up the bed. "Actually," I said, "it was horrid! I wished I hadn't gone."

The Afterthought stared at me, her eyes wide. "Why? What was horrid about it?"

"Everything! The people – Zed. He got *drunk*. And I'm sure there were drugs. It was scary, 'cos they were all heaps older than me, and –" I hugged my knees to my chest "– we didn't stay at the first party, we went on to another one in Croydon, and Zed wouldn't come home, and—"

"Where's Croydon?" said the Afterthought.

"I don't know! Somewhere. On the train. Miles away. And I didn't have my ticket, Zed had it, and I didn't know how to get to the station, and it was really late and I thought Dad would be so worried."

"Dad never worries," said the Afterthought. "Mum would have done."

"Mum would never have let me go in the first place," I said.

"No."

We fell silent, thinking about it. The Afterthought sat back on her heels, looking like a little plump elf in her nightie. For some reason, I don't know why, I suddenly felt fond of her.

"I don't think I *ought* to have gone," I said. "I don't think Dad should have let me."

The Afterthought put her thumb in her mouth and sucked at it.

I said, "Dad lets us do all kinds of things he shouldn't."

"Like what?" said the Afterthought, through a mouthful of thumb.

"Like watching stuff on telly that Mum would say wasn't suitable. Like eating junk food every day. Like driving in the front seat of the car without a seat belt!"

"Mm. But it is *nice* being here with Dad," said the Afterthought. She scrambled out of bed, scooped up Titch from a pile of clothes, and jumped back into bed again. Titch immediately started purring, and kneading with his claws. "If we hadn't come to stay with Dad,"  said the Afterthought, "we wouldn't have had a kitten."

"Would you still like to stay with him all the time?" I said.

The Afterthought considered the question, her head to one side. "*Most* of the time," she said.

"What's that mean?"

"It means I'd stay with Dad in the holidays, 'cos it's more fun with Dad, but I'd stay with Mum during term."

"Then you'd be with Mum longer than you would with Dad," I said.

The Afterthought frowned. "Maybe Mum could come and live in Brighton. That'd be best! Then we could live with either of them, depending how we felt."

"So if we felt like having a good time we'd stay with Dad, and if we felt like being looked after we'd go and stay with Mum."

"Something like that," said the Afterthought. "But Mum would have to come and live in Brighton. We couldn't keep going up to Nottingham."

I said, "Why don't you dream that Dad might win the lottery while you're about it?"

"'Cos he says the chances of winning the lottery are even worse than… something to do with horse racing that I couldn't understand," said the Afterthought.

"Yes," I said, "and the chances of Mum coming to live in Brighton are about nine million to one, so you can forget that idea!"

"In that case, I'll stay with Dad," said the Afterthought; but she didn't sound quite as bullish about it as she had before. I felt she was just saying it.

I wondered what *I* was going to say to Vix, about the party. Unfortunately I had already sent her a card telling her that I was going, otherwise I would probably just have said nothing at all. I knew she wouldn't forget about it as I'd made this really big thing of it. I suppose

I'd boasted, just a little. *Zed has asked me to a party!* She'd be breathlessly waiting to hear what it was like.

I didn't want to lie to her and say it had been brilliant, because if you lie to your best friend it is almost like lying to yourself; and besides, I had this feeling that once I was back home – because we *were* going back home. We had to! – I might want to talk about it with her. On the other hand, I didn't want to admit that I had been a baby and a scaredy cat and a total wimp as I thought she might meet up with Anje or Heidi (our other two friends from school) and just casually mention that "Poor old Steph's been to a horrible druggy party and frightened herself!" and then it would be all round everywhere in next to no time 'cos Anje and Heidi are two of the biggest goss-mongers around. I wouldn't want people like Rhiannon getting to hear of it!

In the end, I just sort of fluffed.

Hi, Vix! I guess you'll be panting to hear all about the party, but there's TOO MUCH TO WRITE on a postcard so you'll just have to contain yourself! Will tell all when I am back. Loadsaluv, Steph.

I also did a postcard for Mum.

Dear Mum, I went to a party Saturday night with this boy I met on the pier. (It is all right, he goes to a POSH SCHOOL.) Dad said I was to be home by midnight but we left the first party and went on to another, so I didn't quite make it!!! It was gone one o'clock when I got in, I know you wouldn't approve, but I came home with other people so I was quite safe. Please don't worry! xxx Stephanie

I suppose I was being a bit sneaky, telling Mum all about the party and about not getting home till one o'clock. I didn't want to get Dad into trouble – though I thought it probably wouldn't matter, now that he and Mum were separated. After all, Mum couldn't do anything to him. She couldn't throw any more frying pans – but I did want Mum to get rattled. I wanted her to fly into one of her panics and snatch up the phone and ring me and say, "Stephanie! I'm catching the first plane back. I want you and your sister to come home *immediately*!"

I wasn't certain how long it took a postcard to get to Spain. A day or two, maybe? I imagined that Mum would probably ring on either Wednesday or Thursday, and I thought that I would keep my mobile with me at all times and make sure (unlike Dad) that the battery was always charged.

Monday morning, Zed rang. He said, "Hi, Passion! Enjoy the party?" Just as if nothing had ever happened! As if he had never had too much to drink and got silly and refused to take me home. But I am such a coward, I didn't say anything. I just meekly mumbled, "Yeah, it was great." The Afterthought, who was sitting on the floor nearby, playing with Titch, looked at me and pulled a face. I pulled one back and whisked myself away into the bedroom. When I came out, a few minutes later, the Afterthought said, "Are you going to see him again?"

I didn't tell her to mind her own business. She wasn't being nosy; it was just sisterly concern. I said, "No. I told him we'd got to go somewhere with Dad."

"Suppose he sees you?" said the Afterthought.

"He won't," I said.

"He might, if we go into town."

"So we won't go into town! We'll stop indoors."

"But there's no food," wailed the Afterthought.

I said in that case we would sneak out and buy some and bring it back with us. The Afterthought liked that idea. She said she didn't particularly want to go out, anyway, because of Titch.

"He'd get lonely, by himself."

I pointed out that people left cats by themselves all

the time, but the Afterthought said not when they were just tiny kittens.

"I wouldn't mind if he had a catty friend… we ought to have got two!"

"You'll be lucky if Mum lets you keep *one*," I said.

"Not going back to Mum," muttered the Afterthought.

I did wish she would stop saying it! It was starting to make me nervous. It worried me that it was such ages since Mum had last rung. It worried me that she'd told Dad she only wanted to be contacted in emergencies. If only I'd asked her about it, last time we'd spoken! But I'd been too busy telling her about all the things we were doing. The Afterthought was convinced that Mum had washed her hands of us.

"She doesn't want us any more! She's given us to Dad."

But I still refused to believe it. Mum wouldn't do such a thing! She just needed a break, without having to consider other people for once in her life. By the end of the holiday she'd be back to normal. At least, that was what I told myself. But every time the Afterthought muttered about "not going back", little niggling doubts began worming their way in.

The one time I'd tried asking Dad, he'd just told me that I worried too much; there didn't seem much point asking him again. Also, I think perhaps I was a bit scared of what he might say, I mean, in case things might have changed. I thought what he would *probably* say would be, "Hang loose, Honeybun! Don't get yourself in a lather." But suppose he didn't? Suppose he said the Afterthought was right? I couldn't cope with that! I didn't want to know.

So I told the Afterthought to just shut up – which somewhat to my surprise she did, which was a bit worrying in itself – and dragged her off down the road to the little shop on the corner, where we stocked up with a day's food.

Coca Cola, Pot Noodles, cheese and onion crisps, Mars bars, Smarties, two apples, a pint of milk and a tin of kitten food.

I got the apples because I felt guilty about not eating our five portions of fresh fruit and vegetables a day, like you're supposed to. Mum always made sure that we did, but since coming to Brighton we'd eaten hardly any fresh fruit or veg at all. It had been nothing but fish and chips and takeaways.

On our way back to Dad's basement we bumped into Ms Devine. She didn't seem as friendly as she had before. She asked me, quite coldly, where Dad was. I said that he was out working.

"Working where, exactly?" said Ms Devine.

I said I didn't know. "He didn't tell us."

"No!" She gave a little snicker, but not like she was amused. "I'm sure he didn't!"

"Would you like me to give him a message?" I said.

"What a good idea! Why not? Just tell him, when he gets back from doing whatever it is he's doing, that my patience is running out. OK?"

I said, "Your patience is running out."

"Right! My patience is running out. He'll understand."

"I don't think I like that lady," said the Afterthought, as Ms Devine went on her way.

I said that when we had first met her I had wondered if she might perhaps be Dad's girlfriend, but now I didn't think she was.

"She might have been," said the Afterthought. "And then Dad might have decided he didn't want her any more, and that's what's made her angry."

I said, "Mm... maybe." But I had a feeling it was something more than that.

When Dad came home that afternoon, I gave him Ms Devine's message.

"Wretched woman," said Dad. He didn't sound particularly bothered.

"Have you thrown her over?" said the Afterthought.

"Have I what?" said Dad.

"Thrown her over... you know! Junked her. Given her the elbow... *jilted* her."

I have no idea how the Afterthought knows these expressions. Dad gave a loud barking laugh and said, "What on earth makes you think that?"

"She sounds like she's mad at you," said the Afterthought.

"Oh! Well." Dad shrugged.

I said, "Did you ever pay her the rent that she wanted?"

"Not yet," said Dad. "I haven't had a chance, she's been away."

"I think she's there now," I said. I'd heard her playing music earlier on. "Maybe if you gave her the rent it would make her happy."

"Oh, she can wait!" said Dad. "She's not short of a bob or two. Let's go out and eat, I've had a hard day."

It seemed that Dad was back in the money, which meant he *must* have been working. I tried asking him where, so that I could tell Ms Devine if she stopped us again, but he just waved a hand and said, "Here and there, round and about... where shall we go for dinner?"

*   *   *

Wc all stayed home next day. I was still scared to go out in case I bumped into Zed, Dad said he didn't have any more work to do just at the moment, and the Afterthought was worried about Titch. She said that he had to have his injections. The lady up the road had said he had to. If he didn't have his injections, he would catch some horrible disease and die.

"We've got to get them done, Dad!"

Dad said we would get them done later, when he had a bit more money.

"But he'll catch something!" wailed the Afterthought.

"He won't catch anything," said Dad. "How can he catch anything when he doesn't go out? Where's he going to catch it from?"

That reminded me of something else. "He needs more litter," I said. "His litter tray's practically empty."

"Yes, and he needs more food, as well," said the Afterthought.

I was beginning to see what Mum meant, about looking after a cat. Titch was only tiny, but he had to eat every day, and he had to have litter, and sooner or later, when he was bigger, he *would* have to have his injections.

Dad grumbled, but he agreed that I could go up the road and get some cat food. He said, however, that litter was a luxury, and we should go into the garden and dig up some earth.

"While I'm getting the cat food," I said, "should I get something for us?"

Dad said yes, but not to go mad. He gave me a £5 note and told me to "spend it sensibly".

"Dinner *and* lunch?" I said. "Or are we going out again?"

"Just get what you can," said Dad. "See how far you can stretch it."

Well! Quite honestly, £5 doesn't stretch all that far. In fact it stretches hardly any way at all. I had to keep adding up in my head as I went round the shelves. One tin of kitten food, one loaf of bread – tin of baked beans – apples! Tomato soup. Cheese. Crisps. Phew! I even got 2p change!

I went racing home with my bag of groceries, thinking that I had done really well and that Mum would have been proud of me. I had managed to buy enough food for three people, not to mention a kitten, and it was *all healthy*.

"Look!" I laid it out, on the table. Dad just grunted. I thought that he seemed preoccupied, like his thoughts were elsewhere. "We can have baked beans for lunch, with apples. Then crisps in the afternoon, if we get hungry. Then for dinner we can have soup followed by bread and cheese." I sat back, triumphantly.

"It's all *veggie*," said the Afterthought.

"Yes, it is," I said. "So what?"

"Why couldn't you have got a TV dinner, or something?"

"'Cos TV dinners cost more and in any case they're *junk*," I said.

"So's crisps," said the Afterthought. "Mum wouldn't let us eat crisps all the time! We had crisps yesterday."

"Well, you have to eat *something*," I said. It was difficult trying to plan a balanced diet without any proper cooking facilities.

"Could have got frankfurters," said the Afterthought.

I said, "Frankfurters are dead pig. You want to eat dead pig?"

She sniffed.

"Just shut up whingeing," I said.

"Could have got sardines!"

"Could have got all sorts of things if we could *cook*!"

Still she went on whingeing. "I don't like baked beans. I don't like tomato soup. Why can't we go out again? Dad, let's go out again!"

"Not tonight," said Dad. "we're staying in tonight."

"We could go on the pier, we could go to that place we went to before, we c—"

"I said, not tonight," said Dad. "We're staying in tonight."

"Couldn't we even get a takeaway?"

"Samantha, I am not made of money," said Dad.

The Afterthought subsided. She went off, muttering to herself, to open a tin for Titch. Titch pranced after her, his tail in the air. He was happy, at any rate. I did think it rather odd that Dad should have enough money to take us out for a meal one day, and the next day claim to be broke. Well, "not made of money". He had obviously been made of money yesterday. What had happened to it all? I thought perhaps he was saving it to give to Ms Devine; it was the only thing that made any sense. But then, at six o'clock, just as I was thinking we ought to eat our soup and bread and cheese, there was a knock at the door and Dad went, like, help, help, hide me! and fled into the bedroom.

"If that's her from upstairs," he said, "tell her I'm out. Tell her I won't be back till late. Tell her I'll pay her the rent tomorrow morning!"

He grabbed the Afterthought and pulled her in with him; in case, I suppose, she gave the game away. Feeling distinctly nervous, I opened the door. Ms Devine was standing there. She looked pretty angry.

"I should like to speak to your father," she said.

"I'm s-sorry." I gulped down a golf ball that seemed to have lodged in my throat. "He's not here."

"Where is he? Do you know?"

I said, "N-no. I'm s-sorry, I don't."

"When is he coming back?"

I gulped at a second golf ball. I am not actually terribly good at telling lies. It's not so much that I think it's wrong, though of course it *is* wrong – well, usually. It's just that I get all embarrassed and tongue-tied. I would be absolutely useless if I ever had to take a lie detector test.

"He won't be b-back till l-l-late," I said. "But he s-said to t-tell you... he'll pay you the rent tomorrow!"

"Oh. Will he?" She was peering past my shoulder, trying to see if she could catch me out.

"He will!" I said. "He will! Tomorrow m-morning. He said!"

"He'd better," said Ms Devine. "*Or else!* Just make sure he gets the message."

With that, she swished back up the steps. I could tell that she had "had it up to here", as Mum would say. Meaning, if she'd had a frying pan to hand, she would most probably have thrown it. Dad gets you like that. I shouldn't be surprised if there aren't people all over England that would like to throw frying pans at him. Except why stop at England? People all over the *world*. All wanting to throw frying pans. I would quite like to have thrown one myself, if there had been one around, though I think, probably, I was more anxious than cross. Dad had gone and upset Ms Devine! He obviously owed her loads and loads of rent, and didn't have enough money to pay it. I had visions of the police coming round and arresting him. Of me and the Afterthought – and Titch – being thrown on to the street, without any money to get back home.

"Dad!" I rushed across to the bedroom. "That was Ms Devine! She said to tell you that you'd better pay the rent, or—"

"Or what?" squeaked the Afterthought.

"Or else!" I said.

"Or else?" The Afterthought's voice had gone all quavery. "What does she mean?"

"She means she's going to kick up," said Dad. "The woman is a menace! She obviously has a very small, grasping mind. Well, there's only one thing for it… the time has come to move on. Don't worry!" He held up a hand. "I've been expecting it. I have it all under control. Everything taken care of, no need to panic. Life's a big adventure, eh?"

He grinned, and chucked me under the chin. I smiled, uncertainly.

"Are we going somewhere?" said the Afterthought.

"Later," said Dad. "When it's dark. Let's eat first. Come along, mother!" He pushed me back into the other room. "Where's our din-dins?"

I remember that evening as being very strange. After we'd eaten dinner, we all settled down to watch television, like nothing was any different from usual. I kept trying to find out from Dad what he was planning to do, where he was planning to take us, but he just shook his head and said, "It'll all work out, don't worry." But I couldn't help worrying! At one point Dad said, "You did bring your passports, didn't you?"

"Dad, we're not going *abroad*?" I said. He'd originally told us to bring them in case we might make a trip over to France. Mum had said, "You'll be lucky!" and up until now Dad hadn't mentioned anything more about it. "We're not going to France?" I said.

"Oh, just a day trip, maybe," said Dad. "I don't know, I haven't decided. But we've got to get out of here!"

"Because of her upstairs?" said the Afterthought.

"Not just her," said Dad. "She's nothing. She's rubbish! I can handle her. But there are... other people. Bad people. People that have got it in for me."

"You mean, like they're... after you?" I quavered.

"After me," said Dad. "Yes! But don't worry! They'll never find us. I've got it all in hand. Big adventure, eh?"

This time, I only managed half a smile, just crimping my mouth at the corners. I wished I could ring Mum! I asked Dad again for her number, but he said, "Stephanie, for heaven's sake! Now is not the time."

"Dad, *please*," I said.

"Stephanie, did you hear what I said? *Now is not the time!*"

"But, D—"

"*STEPHANIE!*"

Dad never shouted at us. Never. So I knew at once that this was serious. It made me even more desperate to ring Mum, but I didn't dare ask him again.

"Steph, I'm sorry," said Dad. "I didn't mean to be cross, sweetheart! But you must understand that there's a time and place for everything, and now is quite definitely not the time to go bothering your mum. What could she do, over there in Spain? You'd just worry her half out of her mind. No! Let's get ourselves settled first."

"Settled w-where?" I said.

Dad tapped a finger to the side of his nose. "Secret venue. Trust me! I've got it all worked out."

Far from making me feel better, this just made me feel worse. Since when did Dad ever have anything *all worked out*?

"When are we going?" said the Afterthought.

"When I say and not before," said Dad. "The less you know, the better."

"Why?" said the Afterthought.

"Because I say so, that's why!"

"Is it so we won't be able to tell them anything if they catch us?"

"If who catch us?" I said.

"The people that are after us!"

"No one's after you," said Dad. "It's me they've got it in for, not you. Now just sit down and keep quiet. Read a book, or something. Watch the telly!"

We watched television right through till nearly midnight. The Afterthought had long since fallen asleep, curled into a corner of the sofa with Titch. I was too worried to sleep. I didn't quite know what was going on, but whatever it was, I knew it wasn't anything good. When Dad said people were after him, I didn't think he meant people with frying pans, and I didn't think they were after him simply because he had got up their noses. I remembered the day he had shown us his wad, a great fistful of money. I couldn't help wondering where it had all come from – and where it had all gone. I didn't think Dad would have stolen it; I didn't think he was a thief.

But it was very peculiar how he could have all that money one day, and none the next. What could he be doing with it?

And then I thought of Mum's cooker money, and the way Dad had lost it all on the horses. I thought of the time he had taken us out for a champagne dinner, when he had *won* money on the horses. And I knew, I just knew, with horrible certainty, that Dad hadn't been going to work all those times, he'd been going to the race track, or to the betting office, and now he had done something really stupid and upset some really bad people, and they were coming after him, and we were all in danger. Big adventure, eh? But I don't think I'm a very adventurous sort of person, because all I wanted was to be back at home with Mum, safe and sound in Nottingham.

At midnight, Dad switched off the telly and said, "Right, girls! This is it... time to go. Wake up, sleeping beauty!"

He told us both to pack all our stuff and make ready to leave. The Afterthought was worried about Titch.

"He hasn't got a carrying case!"

Dad said not to bother about a carrying case, just put him in the car and keep an eye on him, but the Afterthought wouldn't. She said it wasn't safe, he could escape and get run over. Dad made impatient clicking noises with his tongue, but the Afterthought can be stubborn. When she digs her heels in, there's no moving her. Dad knew this. He said, "Oh, for God's sake!" and snatched up a cardboard box that we had once brought groceries home in. "Punch some holes in this and shove him inside. And be quick about it!"

But the Afterthought wouldn't be hurried; not where her precious kitten was concerned. I can't say I blame her. I helped her make some air holes, and settle Titch inside, and then we bound it round with a belt to make it secure. Dad, who was fretting and fuming at the door, said, "All right, all right, that'll do! Let's get moving."

He told us to go up the steps "like little mice" and open the car "as quiet as can be". He practically threw us into the back, all higgledy-piggledy with our bags and packages. He said we'd stop when we got out of town and transfer stuff to the boot.

"There's no time right now. We have to get away!"

"We're not going to run out of petrol, are we?" I said.

"No, we're not," said Dad. "Don't be cheeky!"

I wasn't being; I was genuinely frightened. I imagined all the bad people coming after us in fast cars, with guns, and us suddenly grinding to a halt as we had before. But this time, it seemed, Dad was prepared. He had obviously been planning his getaway and had filled up the tank in readiness.

"I told you … trust me! I know what I'm doing."

I wished I could believe him. I wished I could speak to Mum! But I couldn't, and there was nothing I could do.

We drove and drove, all through the night. The Afterthought went to sleep again, and after a bit I slept, too. I'd meant to stay awake and  watch where we were going, but in the end I couldn't stop my eyes from closing. When I opened them again, it was just getting light.

"Are we here?" said the Afterthought.

"We're here," said Dad. "Now, I want you to be very quiet or we'll wake people up. Just remember, it's still early. OK?"

We nodded.

"OK! Grab your stuff and let's get you indoors."

We staggered out of the car and followed Dad up some steps to a block of flats. I wanted to ask where we were, but I didn't get a chance. Dad had pressed the intercom and a man's voice was crackling at us. "Daniel? That you?"

"Yeah, it's me," said Dad.

There was the sound of a buzzer, and Dad pushed the door open and shepherded us through, into an entrance hall. There was a lift, but Dad took us up the stairs. At the top of the first flight a man was waiting for us. I have tried and tried to remember what he looked like, but I only just saw him the once; and, besides, everything was so weird and confusing, and I was still half asleep from the drive.

The man asked Dad if everything had gone OK, and Dad said yes, fine. He said he would just get me and the Afterthought bedded down, then go and see to the car, but the man said to give him the keys and *he* would see to it. I don't know what he meant by "see to it", but it didn't seem to be there any more after that. Not as far as I could tell, though I really couldn't tell very much.

We didn't go out again for the next few days.

# nine

WE LIVED IN this one room. It was a bedroom, and at least it had a double bed, which was something to be thankful for. Me and the Afterthought shared the bed; I don't know where Dad slept, but I think it was on the sofa, outside, because once when I went to the bathroom I saw the cushions all rumpled, and a dent in one of them like a head had been lying there.

The only times Dad would let us leave the bedroom were if we needed to go to the loo, and then we had to ask him first. I think he wanted to make sure that we didn't bump into anyone. We weren't ever allowed into the rest of the flat – in case, I suppose, we poked around and saw something we shouldn't, like a name and address, or telephone number, or something – so we never got to see the man again. The one who'd met us on the stairs.

Dad said, "Trust me! It's for your own good."

At night he locked us in. It was so embarrassing, he gave us a *bucket*. He tried making jokes about it.

"Slopping out, that's what they call it in the nick… pretend you're making a movie! You're a couple of bank robbers, and you've been banged up. Prison movie! Right?"

I said, "Right!" and tried to smile. But it wasn't funny. We felt we really *were* in prison.

"Oh, come on, now, cheer up!" said Dad. "It's not as bad as all that. It's not like you're in for a ten-year stretch… with time off for good behaviour, you'll be out before you know it. Couple of days! Three at the most. Surely you can manage that for your old dad?"

Actually, it was five days. Five whole days, shut up in one room! Apart from a big dramatic scene – Don't look! And *don't listen*! – every time she had to use the bucket, the Afterthought coped with it better than I did. She said she didn't mind where she was, so long as she was with Dad.

"After all, I've got Titch," she said.

At least Dad got Titch some proper cat litter. *That* was a relief. But I discovered that I suffer from this thing where I don't like to be locked up. I know now how animals must feel in zoos. I think zoos are just so *cruel*. I won't ever go to one again. Not unless the animals are allowed to roam about. I couldn't roam anywhere, and I began to have these nightmares that Dad had gone mad and we would be kept locked up for ever.

We weren't even supposed to look out of the windows in case somebody saw us. I tried, once, just lifting up the edge of the blind, and the Afterthought nearly went berserk. She yelled at me to "Get away, get away!" She thought the bad guys might be out there, watching.

"How would they know who we were?" I said.

The Afterthought said they would know because they would have cased the joint. (She picks up this sort of language. She is like a magpie.) She said they would have spied on us in Brighton. They would know that we belonged to Dad, and they would guess that if we were here, Dad would also be here, and then they would come and get him. She was really quite scared, so after that I didn't try looking out of the window any more. Partly because I didn't want to upset the Afterthought, and partly because – well, because I thought she just *could* be right. I didn't want anything happening to Dad.

"What's out there, anyway?" said the Afterthought.

I said, "Nothing very much. Just garages."

Dad did his best to keep us occupied. We had a television, and we played lots of games, like going through the alphabet with pop stars, movie stars, TV programmes. We played card games – Dad taught us how to play poker! – and pencil and paper games, and Scrabble and Monopoly, on a very old Monopoly board that was falling to pieces. Dad also brought us books and

magazines – including the one that Mum wouldn't let me read. I asked him to get it for me, not thinking that he would, but he didn't seem to see anything wrong with it, or maybe he just picked it off the shelf without really looking. The only thing was, I couldn't enjoy it properly. I opened it up, looking forward to a good wallow, and all I could think of was… Mum! How I was deliberately going behind her back. Reading stuff she didn't approve of. I mean, like, normally it wouldn't have bothered me, I'd have thought "Sah, sah, and sucks to Mum!" But now it just seemed like I was being disloyal.

The day after we arrived I tried ringing home on my mobile, but there wasn't any reply and I couldn't leave a message as we didn't have an answer phone. (We do now.) I then tried Vix, but she obviously wasn't back from holiday yet. I left a bit of a message, just saying that we weren't in Brighton any more and I'd ring her later, or she could ring me when she got back, but it wasn't the same as actually talking to her. I needed to talk to someone!

"There's nobody around," I said. I collapsed, dispiritedly, on to the bed. "I can't get anyone!"

"You shouldn't be phoning people, anyway," said the Afterthought. "The line could be bugged. They could be *listening*."

By "they" she meant the bad guys. The Afterthought had become obsessed by bad guys. At night she was terrified of going to sleep in case they broke into the flat with machine guns. I told her there was no way anyone could have bugged my mobile. I mean, there probably was, because what do I know about these things? But I didn't want her totally freaking out. I said that just ringing Mum or Vix couldn't do any harm.

"It could if they traced the call," said the Afterthought.

"Not if I only speak for a few seconds," I said. "They wouldn't be able to trace it." I had seen enough police series to know that much.

The Afterthought still wasn't convinced. "They'd know who you were calling! They might go and get Mum and beat her up."

I said, "What would they do that for?"

"To find out where Dad is!"

"But she wouldn't know where Dad is! *We* don't even know where we are."

The Afterthought sucked at her thumb. "She might go to the police."

I had already thought of that. Maybe, at the back of my mind, it was what I was hoping for. I wouldn't do it myself, because that would be betraying Dad; it could get him into a whole lot of trouble. I still didn't know what he'd done, exactly, or where he'd got his money from, but I had this uneasy feeling that it might be something not quite legal. I wouldn't want to be the one who got him into trouble! I didn't care how oddly he was behaving, he was still my dad, and I still loved him. But if Mum were to ring the police – well! There wasn't much I could do about that.

"Do you honestly think she would?" I said.

"Yes! 'Cos if you told her we weren't in Brighton any more she'd want to know where we'd gone, and if you said you didn't know she'd get really mad and tell the police that they'd got to find us, and then Dad would get into trouble *big* time for running away without paying the rent!"

"That would be better than the bad guys getting him," I said.

"It wouldn't, 'cos they'd put him in prison!"

"But at least he'd be safe," I said.

"He wouldn't!" The Afterthought shook her head, violently. "They could still get at him! They could get at him in prison, it's what they do!" I wasn't the only one who'd seen police series. The Afterthought knew all about bad guys and what they got up to. "I don't think you ought to ring *anybody*," she said.

As it happened, I didn't have the chance. Next time I tried (shut away in the bathroom, where no one could hear me) I discovered that I had run out of credit. And I didn't have another phone card! That is the trouble with mobiles; they can let you down. I once saw this movie where some poor woman was having her house broken into by a gang and she was shut in the loo trying to ring for help and she couldn't because her phone was dead. Really scary.

I was starting to get a bit scared, too. There were moments when I actually, almost, felt really *frightened.*

It wasn't so much the thought of the bad guys, nor did I truly believe that Dad had gone mad, but I was desperately worried about how we were ever going to get home, especially now I didn't have my phone. I asked Dad next day, without too much hope, if I could get my credit topped up. He said, "Why? Who do you want to call?"

The Afterthought said, "She's trying to ring Mum! I told her not to. I told her it wasn't safe!"

"I'm afraid Sam's right," said Dad. "I'm sorry, poppet! I know it's not easy for you, cooped up here, but it won't be for much longer. Promise! Just give it another forty-eight hours, and we'll be out."

"Are we going back to Brighton?" said the Afterthought.

"Not on your life! We're going somewhere far more exciting than Brighton."

"Where are we going?" I said.

"Would you believe, the South of France?" said Dad. He announced it with a big happy grin. I stared at him, in dismay.

"The South of *France*?" I said.

"Nice, to be exact," said Dad. "You've heard of Nice?" I nodded. "You'll love it down there!"

"But… what about Mum?" I said.

"Stephie, love, face it," said Dad. "You're with me, now. Your mum—" he waved a hand. "It's not that she doesn't love you any more, but – well! She feels it's time to make a new life for herself."

There was this moment of absolute silence. I think even the Afterthought was a bit stunned. She didn't even try saying *I told you so*.

"You mean…" I could feel my voice starting to crack. "You mean, she *really* doesn't want us back?"

"Oh, I'm sure! For holidays," said Dad.

"N-not to s-stay?"

"Well, yes, like you've stayed with me."

"But not to *live*?"

"See, it's like this," said Dad. "Your mum feels she's done her stint. Now it's my turn. That's all right, isn't it? It's not so bad, being with your dad?"

Stupidly, I said, "But what about s-school?"

"Find you a new one. Go to a French one!"

"But I don't speak French!"

"Soon learn," said Dad. "You'll probably learn faster than me. Now, come on, cheer up! Happy face! It'll be fun! Life's a big adventure, eh? Sam wants to come with me, don't you? She loves her old dad!"

"Don't you at least think we ought to – to ring Mum and ask her?" I said.

"I've already asked her," said Dad. "She's given us her blessing."

I was, like, gob-smacked. I couldn't believe it! I couldn't believe that even Dad would do such a thing. He had gone behind my back! Spoken to Mum without telling me! Why hadn't he let *me* speak to her?

"When did you do it?" I said.

"Oh! A few days ago. Just before we left Brighton."

"Why didn't you tell us?" I screamed.

"Sorry, poppet! Didn't mean to upset you."

Dad reached out to give me a hug, but I wriggled away from him. I didn't feel like being hugged. I felt hurt, and angry, and betrayed. He was treating us the same way he'd treated Mum all those years, making decisions without consulting her, doing things he knew she wouldn't approve of. Then saying sorry and expecting to be forgiven.

"Stephie, Stephie! Don't be cross." Just like with Mum! "My main concern," said Dad, "was to get you girls safely away. We were in a lot of danger, you know. I couldn't bear it if anything had happened to you!"

I thought to myself that if Dad was so worried about me and the Afterthought, he shouldn't have got mixed up with the bad guys in the first place.

"Now she hates me," said Dad.

"I don't hate you," I said. "But I don't want to go to France!"

"Ah, Steph, you'll love it once you're there!"

"You will," said the Afterthought. Her hand stole into mine. "You will, Steph! Honest!"

The Afterthought seemed to be OK with the idea now that she had had time to get used to it. Me, I was sunk in gloom. It is really upsetting to be told that your mum doesn't want you any more. I knew we had both been mean to her, but I had never, ever thought she would get rid of us. I didn't want to go to France! I didn't want to go to a French school, I didn't want to speak French. I wanted to go home, to my mum! And there was something I didn't understand. If Dad hadn't had the money to pay Ms Devine her rent, how come he had the money to take us all to Nice? If he really *did* have the money to take us to Nice.

I put this to him, and he laughed. "I've got money! You surely don't think I'd be irresponsible enough to let you join me on my travels if I didn't have the means to look after you?"

I knew what Mum would say. But Mum wasn't there. She didn't care!

"If you've got money," I said – I said it quite carefully, not wanting Dad to think I was having a go at him – "couldn't you have paid Ms Devine her rent?"

"Oh, look, just forget about Ms Devine!" Dad sprang

up and began pacing the room. "She's loaded, she doesn't need it. You don't want to waste your time feeling sorry for people like her. As far as they're concerned, we're just scum. They wouldn't give us the snot out their noses! I've had to work hard for this lot."

 Dad patted a hand on a case that he had brought with him. One of those smooth, flat sort of ones that people snap open in movies to reveal bundles of notes. Did Dad's contain bundles of notes?

"I've put my life on the line for this! Why should I give any to the likes of her?"

"She was hateful, anyway," said the Afterthought. "She didn't deserve it!"

"Precisely," said Dad. "So don't let's shed any more crocodile tears for Ms Devine. I have you two girls to care for. You're far more important to me than she is!"

I still felt that it was wrong of Dad not to pay her the money, but I didn't try arguing. Dad hated being argued with; he always said it was a form of nagging. Mum used to argue all the time. It was one of Dad's worst accusations, to say that either of us was "starting to get like your mum". Not that he ever really said it to the Afterthought. She didn't argue. She thought whatever Dad did had got to be OK.

177

"Ms Devine's got a *whole house*," she said, as we lay in bed that night. "Dad hasn't got anything!"

"Still doesn't make it right," I muttered.

"Oh, stop sounding like Mum!" said the Afterthought. She'd picked it up from Dad; she knew he used it as an insult.

"At least Mum doesn't run away without paying people what she owes them," I said.

"Mum doesn't need to! She's got things. She's got a house, she's got a job, sh—"

"Yes, and how is Dad going to look after us when he hasn't got *anything*?" I said. "He hasn't got a house, he hasn't got a job… how's he going to earn money?"

"Dad can earn money," said the Afterthought.

"He can *get* money," I said.

"It's the same thing!"

"It's not," I said. It wasn't the same thing at all. I thought of the case he had showed us. The flat case with the snap locks, like you see on the movies. I sat up, and crawled to the end of the bed.

"What are you doing?" said the Afterthought.

The case was sitting there, on top of the dressing table. I reached out for it.

"That's Dad's!" shrilled the Afterthought.

Yes, it was – and I wanted to find out what was inside it. But I couldn't! It wouldn't open; it had one of those special combination locks. It did feel quite heavy, though. How much money could you get in a case like that? Hundreds? Thousands?

"Stephanie, put it back!" said the Afterthought. "It's nothing to do with us."

I had the feeling that in spite of her bravado, the Afterthought was actually a bit nervous. She really didn't want to know what was in the case.

"I think Dad got this from gambling," I said.

"So what?" said the Afterthought. "People are allowed to gamble!"

"Yes, but it's not the same as earning it… it's not like doing a proper job. And why are we having to run away?"

"Because of the bad guys!"

"But why? What do they want? Why are they after us? Because it's their money, maybe. Because Dad—" I didn't want to say because Dad had stolen it from them; I refused to think my dad was a thief. But perhaps… perhaps he had been too clever for them?

"I'm going to sleep," said the Afterthought. She scooped up Titch, and put him into bed. "I don't want to talk about it!"

I didn't want to talk about it, either, but I felt that I had to say *something*. To Dad, I mean. I wasn't brave enough to ask him where the money had come from, but I did think I needed to know what was going to happen to us once it had run out.

"Quite right!" said Dad. He had brought in our breakfast tray next morning, plus a little saucer of cat food for Titch. "A sensible question. I'm glad you asked it! I did tell you, didn't I, that I wouldn't take you with me if I couldn't provide for you?"

"Dad, you're not going to – to *gamble*?" I whispered.

Dad laughed; this big hearty laugh. "Oh, Stephie, Stephie, you grow more like your mum every day! No, I'm not going to gamble – at least, not for a living. I might have a little flutter on the gee-gees just now and again. You wouldn't begrudge me that, would you?"

Numbly, I shook my head.

"That's all right, then! I couldn't lead a totally joyless existence. Got to have a bit of fun, eh?"

He winked at the Afterthought, who beamed and nodded.

"Good! Right. Now, you'll be happy to hear –" Dad rubbed his hands together "– that today is the day… we're up and off! So, it's a question of finishing your breakfast, getting yourselves packed, and we'll be on our way."

The Afterthought instantly began cramming food into her mouth as fast as she could go. Dad, amused, said, "No need to choke yourself!"

He still hadn't answered my question.

"Dad," I said.

"Mm?"

I took a deep breath. "What *are* you going to do?"

"What am I going to do? I'll tell you what I'm going to do! First off, I'm going to find us somewhere to stay, and then I'm going to pay a visit to an old chum who runs a casino."

"Casino like on the pier?" said the Afterthought.

"Casino like in Las Vegas," said Dad. "Bright lights, diamond tiaras – and money, money, money!"

"I thought you said you weren't going to gamble!" I cried.

"*I'm* not going to gamble," said Dad. "Other people are. Your dad's going to be a—"

I thought he said "croopyer", but have since discovered it's spelt *croupier*. It's one of those people that stand at gaming tables with a sort of rake thing, raking in the money and pushing little piles of it back to you if you've hit the winning number.

"What do you think of that?" said Dad.

He sounded so proud of himself! He'd got a real job to go to – or would have, once he'd seen his friend.

"Don't worry! It's there, waiting for me."

"See? I told you," said the Afterthought, as we packed up our stuff yet again. "I told you Dad would take care of us!"

And then it came time to leave. I grabbed our bags, while the Afterthought cradled Titch, in his makeshift carry box.

"Oh – um – Sam," said Dad. "I meant to say, earlier… you'd better leave Titch here."

*Leave Titch?* The Afterthought froze. I could see Dad knew at once he was treading dangerously. No power on earth would separate the Afterthought from her beloved kitten.

"He'll be looked after," pleaded Dad; but the Afterthought just clutched at her box, standing stock-still and mutinous in the middle of the room.

"All right, all right, bung him in the car! But get a move on."

Dad was starting to grow edgy, like he thought the bad guys might jump him if we didn't leave immediately. We bundled ourselves downstairs and into a green car parked out front. It wasn't the car Dad had had before. The Afterthought squeaked, "Oh! It's different."

"I thought Stephanie would like seat belts," said Dad. "Come on, in you get! Quick, quick!"

I wondered if we were going to drive all the way down to the south of France. I thought that Mum wouldn't be very happy about it. She always used to say that Dad was a menace on the roads because a) he drove too fast and b) he never took any notice of road signs. Dad used to say that Mum was even more of a menace.

"Crawling along at 30mph, holding up the flow of traffic… it's people like you that cause accidents!"

As usual, the Afterthought always sided with Dad. She liked going at 60mph and shooting the lights. I guess I am a bit more of a wimp. Nervously I said, "Dad, are we *driving* to Nice?" I was quite relieved when Dad said we were getting a plane.

I still didn't know where we were, but after a while I began to see signs that said Luton and I guessed that we were heading for Luton Airport. We had been there once before, when we had gone on holiday. I couldn't decide whether I was scared or excited. I think I still couldn't quite believe that it was happening.

"Dad," I said, "couldn't we *please* ring Mum before we leave? *Please*, Dad? *Please*?"

"Stephanie, I told you, we'll ring her when we get there," said Dad. "That's a promise! We don't have time, right now. We've got a plane to catch."

"It'll be all right," whispered the Afterthought. "Dad'll take care of us."

I wished I could have as much faith in Dad as my little sister did.

We parked the car in the long-stay car park. I wondered what was going to happen to it, but Dad said his friend who owned the flat would come and get it.

"All taken care of! Don't worry. Now, Sammie, sweetheart, listen to me! About the kitten." I could see the Afterthought stiffen. I thought, so much for her faith in Dad. "You cannot take him over to France. OK? Just can't be done! So be a good girl, and let me have him—" Dad reached out his hands for the box. The Afterthought, immediately, backed away. "Come on, come on! Don't be silly," said Dad. "I haven't got time for all this! Give me the box."

"No!" The Afterthought shot round the other side of the car. "I'm not going without Titch!"

"I told you," said Dad. "There's no way you can bring him. We haven't made arrangements – we haven't even got a proper carrying cage."

"Then I'm not going!"

"Oh, for crying out loud!" Dad raced round the car and made a grab for the box. "Why you couldn't just have left him in the flat—"

"I'm not leaving him anywhere! I'm not leaving him!"

"Dad, you can't just *dump* him," I said.

"I'm not going to dump him, for God's sake! We'll leave him in the car. He'll be picked up in a couple of hours."

Dad made another lunge. The Afterthought scuttled for safety behind me.

"It's no use," I said. "She won't go without him."

"Oh, now, Stephanie, don't you start! You know perfectly well they won't let a cat on the plane."

It seemed to me that Dad should have thought of that before.

"Maybe you'd better go without us," I said.

"Don't be ridiculous! How can I go without you? I can't just go off and leave you here!"

"No, and I'm not just going off and leaving Titch here!" cried the Afterthought.

"*Samantha*—" Dad made one last snatch at the box. This time, he managed to get his hands on it. He wrenched – and the box fell to the ground. Titch let out a piteous wail.

"There, now! Leave him," said Dad. "Stephanie, open that car door and put him back in. And you!" He seized

185

the Afterthought by the arm. "Get a move on! We don't have all day."

That was Dad's BIG mistake. The Afterthought did as she always did in moments of crisis: she went into overdrive. Her piercing shrieks rang through the car park. "The screaming hab dabs" was what Mum used to call it. The Afterthought was an expert. When she was little she used to make a habit of it. She specially liked to do it in places where there were crowds of people, such as shopping malls – and car parks. Mum was the only one who could handle her when she got like that. Dad had never been able to cope. Dad was one of those people, he always turned his back on trouble. Which was what he did now.

"Oh, for God's sake!" he shouted.

Next thing I knew, he was striding off across the car park with his caseful of money, leaving me and the Afterthought on our own, with Titch.

Dad's voice came bellowing back to us: "Just don't say I didn't try!"

# ten

ALL THE TIME the Afterthought was screaming, people were stopping to stare at us. *What is the matter with that child? Why is she making all that noise?* But the minute Dad walked away and the Afterthought calmed down, they all immediately went back to doing their own thing. It was like suddenly we weren't there. We stood by the car, with me clutching Titch, and no one took the slightest notice of us. I'm not sure what I would have expected, but I think perhaps I might have expected someone to ask us if we were OK, or something. Maybe they thought Dad would be coming back for us. It's what I thought, just at first. I really couldn't believe that he would just walk off and leave us.

I balanced Titch on the wing of the car, 'cos his carry box was quite heavy, and told the Afterthought that we would wait where we were.

"I'm not leaving Titch!" said the Afterthought.

I quickly reassured her before she could get herself all worked up again. I had this idea that Dad would come back and say he'd made arrangements for Titch to come with us. Or, alternatively, he would say that we had better all go back to the flat and we would catch another flight in a day or so, *after* he'd made arrangements for Titch to come with us. But he didn't. He didn't do either of those things. We waited and waited, and he never came. The Afterthought slid her hand into mine.

"What are we going to do?" She tugged at me. *"Stephanee! What are we going to do?"*

I thought, this is how it was at the beginning, when we arrived in London and Dad wasn't there. It had been up to me, then, to get us safely on the train for Brighton. Now it seemed it was up to me again – except that this time we didn't have any train tickets, and we didn't have any money, and it wasn't any use the Afterthought asking me what we were going to do because I didn't know!

"I want Mum," said the Afterthought. "Stephanie, I want Mum!"

I wanted Mum, too. I wanted her more than I'd ever wanted anything in the whole of my life!

"Ring her!" said the Afterthought. "Ring her, Steph!"

"What if she's still in Spain?"

"She can't be!"

But she could be. If what Dad had said was true – if Mum really *had* decided to make a new life for herself—

"*Stephanee!*"

"Yes, all right, all right!" I said. "I'll try." And then I remembered. "We haven't got any money!"

"We don't need money," said the Afterthought. "We can reverse the charges. *Please*, Steph! It's what Mum would tell us to do."

"But what if—" I was about to say, what if Mum wasn't there? But I looked down at the Afterthought's face, all puckered up with anxiety, and I sniffed and wiped my eyes on the back of my hand, and did my best to pull myself together. My little sister was relying on me. So was Titch. They were both waiting for me to do something.

"OK!" I picked up the carry box. "Let's go and find a phone."

"You have to dial the operator," said the Afterthought.

I said, "Yes, I know."

"And then they ask the person you're ringing if they'll pay for the call, and—"

"Yes," I said, "I *know*. Bring the bags!"

I tried not to think what we would do if Mum wasn't there. We would have to ring Gran, or Auntie Jenny. But

Gran was old, and in a home, and Auntie Jenny and Mum weren't the hugest of friends. Not since Auntie Jenny had said Dad was a con man, and Mum had taken exception. But we would have to ring someone! Or go to the police.

The police would want to know what had happened. We would have to tell them everything, and that meant Dad would get into trouble. They might even arrest him. I wondered how I felt about that, and decided that I simply didn't care. Dad deserved to be arrested! Abandoning the Afterthought was the meanest thing he had ever done. I didn't mind so much for myself – well, I pretended I didn't – but the Afterthought was his number one fan. She had always stuck up for him and taken his side. She had trusted him, and he had let her down, just like he had let Mum down. Just like he always let everyone down.

If Mum is not there, I thought, I am *definitely* going to the police.

I said this to the Afterthought, expecting her to scream, "Stephanie, no!" But she just nodded and said, "OK."

"We'll try Mum first," I said.

"Yes," said the Afterthought. "Try Mum first."

We found a phone and I dialled the operator and told her the number, and then I looked at the Afterthought and crossed my fingers, and she crossed hers, on both

190

hands, and together we held our breath. And then Mum's voice came on the line!

"Stephanie?" she shrieked. "Is that you? Is Sam with you? Are you all right? Where are you? Where have you been? I've been going frantic!"

I said that the Afterthought was with me and that we were at Luton Airport. Mum's voice rose to a screech.

"Luton Airport? What are you doing at Luton Airport?"

"Dad was going to take us to France," I said, "but we—"

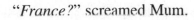

"*France?*" screamed Mum.

"Yes, but we – we decided we didn't want to go with him, and the Afterthought threw one of her tantrums and Dad got scared and now he's gone off and we're stuck here and – oh, Mum! Can we come home?"

"Can you come home? Oh, God, Stephie, of course you can come home! What do you think? I've been waiting here for you! I've been having nightmares, I've been ringing and ringing… get yourselves back here immediately!"

"We can't, we haven't any money," I wailed.

"He's left you without *money*? Oh, for God's sake! I'll wring that man's neck! All right, listen to me. I want you to go *at once* and find a Help desk. Can you do that? Are you inside the actual airport? OK! Go to the nearest Help desk and explain that you're stranded. Right? Tell them that your mum is on her way to pick you up. I'll be there as soon as I can! In the meantime, just sit tight. Don't move, don't talk to anyone. Just wait there for me. You got that?"

I said, "Yes, Mum."

"And if by any chance your dad comes back—"

"I don't think he will," I said.

"If he *does*," said Mum, "and tries to take you anywhere, on no account are you to go with him! Scream the place down, if necessary, but *don't let him take you anywhere.* Promise me, Stephanie!"

I promised, I gave her my solemn word, but Mum still wasn't satisfied. She seemed to think Dad might come waltzing back and carry us off. She told me yet again that we must sit tight and not move, and not go anywhere with anyone, and especially not with Dad.

"I mean it! Don't even go and have a cup of tea with him! Promise me!"

"Mum," I said, "I promise!"

"I shan't know a moment's peace till I have you back! These last forty-eight hours have been the worst of my entire life!"

She was back again, doing her old mumsy thing, and I was just so relieved!

"Mum's coming to fetch us," I said to the Afterthought. "She'll be here as soon as she can."

It was such a weight off my mind, knowing that Mum was on her way and that she hadn't washed her hands of us. It meant we could both stop being frightened for the first time since Dad had told us about the bad guys and whisked us off to our prison cell. I realised, now, that I *had* been frightened, even though I'd kept telling myself that it was OK because we were with Dad. It hadn't been OK at all!

The Afterthought, I must say, has the most amazing powers of recuperation. As soon as she had assured herself that Mum really did want us – "Really, *really*?" – she lost her puckered little anxious frown and went straight back to being her normal bumptious self. Quite extraordinary! She seemed to have totally forgotten that only a few minutes ago she had been clinging to me and whimpering.

The people at the airport, the ones who looked after us until Mum came, thought she was hilarious. She had them in stitches, telling them all about Titch and the things he got up to, imitating his tinny little voice, imitating the way he washed himself, the way he clapped his paws together as he jumped into the air, the way he rubbed himself round you. I suppose she was quite funny, but I am used to her being funny so I just sat back and let her get on with it. I was mainly just happy that I didn't have to be in charge any more.

They looked after us really well, the airport people. They fed us and bought us magazines and even gave us a little saucer of milk for Titch. The Afterthought was worried about him being shut up for so long, so a lady said to let him out and she would guard the door so he couldn't escape. Then the Afterthought started worrying in case he wanted to go to the toilet, so this same kind lady shredded a newspaper into a filing tray and told the Afterthought to put him in there. Titch thought it was great fun. He didn't go to the toilet, but he scattered a lot of newspaper!

In spite of everyone being so nice to us, and the Afterthought showing off like crazy, I couldn't wait to be back with Mum. The moment when I saw her coming towards us was THE VERY BEST MOMENT OF MY ENTIRE LIFE. The Afterthought shrieked, "Mum!" and hurled herself at her. I suddenly felt a bit shy, which I suppose sounds rather silly. I mean, how can you be shy with your own mum? But I am not as madly outgoing as the Afterthought. Then Mum cried, "Stephie!" and held out her arms and I just *fell* into them.

"Oh, God! I've been so worried about you!" Mum hugged us both like she wasn't ever going to let us go again. "What happened to your phone? Did you forget to re-charge it?"

I told her how I had run out of credit and how I couldn't get topped up because of Dad being scared the bad guys might trace any calls that I made. The Afterthought told her about being locked up in one room for five days and having to go to the toilet in a bucket. Mum listened in growing horror as we poured it all out, every last detail.

"Your dad told you *what*?" she said.

"He told us you didn't want us any more. He said that's what you'd said."

"No way!" cried Mum. "All I said was it was his turn to shoulder the burden. But I didn't mean permanently! I just needed a bit of a break."

"He said he'd asked you if it was OK if we went to live in France, and you'd said it was."

"Nothing of the kind!" Mum sounded really angry; almost more angry than I'd ever heard her. Angrier, even, than when she threw the frying pan. "He never said anything about France! A day trip; that was all he ever mentioned. Nothing about you going to live with him! That is total fantasy! He knew perfectly well I would never have agreed."

So Dad had actually lied to us. Probably about other things, as well.

"He wouldn't let me ring you," I said.

"Of course he wouldn't! He knew I'd go straight to the police." Mum raked her fingers through her hair. "Girls, I am so sorry! This is all my fault. I should never have let you go!"

"You needed a break," I said. "We were so mean to you!"

"You were a bit tiresome," agreed Mum. "But you had every right to be! Parents behaving badly… your dad and I were a real disaster area."

"It was Dad," said the Afterthought, "not you!"

"Oh, Sammie!" Mum hugged her. "That's a sweet thing to say! Does it mean you're not cross with me any more!"

"I won't ever be cross with you again!" said the Afterthought, wrapping both arms round Mum's neck.

"You'd better not make promises you can't keep," said Mum. "And by the way," she said, as I picked up Titch in his carry box, "what is that?"

The Afterthought said, "It's Titch! He's my kitten."

"Dad let her have it," I said. "She pestered him until he gave way."

"Hmph!" said Mum.

"Mum, I can keep him, can't I?" The Afterthought unwrapped herself and peered anxiously into Mum's face. "*Please*, Mum! Say that I can!"

"I suppose you'll have to," said Mum, "now that you've got him. I just hope he gets on with—" She stopped.

"With who?" I said.

"I'll tell you later. Oh, dear!" Mum gave an odd little laugh, which sounded more like she was about to burst into tears. "This is terrible! I'm in such a state I'd probably say yes to anything."

"It's 'cos of Titch we didn't go to France," said the Afterthought.

"Not *just* because of Titch," I said, quickly.

"Yes, it was! 'Cos Dad wouldn't let us take him."

"You mean, if you could have taken Titch, you would have gone quite willingly?" said Mum.

"No!" I kicked out, crossly, at the Afterthought.

Stupid insensitive child! "We thought we *had* to go. We didn't want to! But Dad said you were going to make a new life for yourself."

"*That man,*" said Mum. And then she stopped and bit her lip, because I think maybe she had been on the point of saying something really bad. About Dad, I mean. In some ways, in spite of everything, I don't think Mum has ever quite learnt to stop loving him.

"Let's go home," she said.

Home! That sounded so good. But there was something that was niggling at me. Something Mum had said. In the end, I just had to ask her.

"Mum, you know what you said just now?" I said. "About Titch getting on with—" I waved a hand. "Whoever."

"Yes," said Mum.

"You didn't mean… Romy, did you?"

"*Romy?*" The Afterthought bawled it at about a thousand decibels. "You're not going to *marry* him?"

"What if she was?" I said. "We wouldn't mind, Mum! Honest." Not even if he did have ginger hairs up his nose. I wouldn't ever begrudge Mum anything, ever again!

"Mum, *are* you?" said the Afterthought.

"Well, I have no plans right at this moment," said Mum. "But I'll certainly bear it in mind… it's always nice to have your approval!"

There was a pause.

"But if you didn't mean Romy—" I said.

"Which I didn't," said Mum.

What *did* she mean? She wouldn't tell us! It wasn't till we got home that we discovered Mum's secret.

"There you are," said Mum. "What you were clamouring for... I think I must be going soft in the head."

She'd got us a kitten! A dear little stripey one, even tinier than Titch.

"I booked him before I went away," said Mum. "He'd just been born. He was going to be your coming-home present."

"Can't he still be?" begged the Afterthought. "Can't we have two?"

"Oh, have as many as you like!" said Mum. "I told you, I'm so relieved to have you back safe and sound I'd say yes to almost anything... just make the most of it, because I can assure you it won't last! Yes, yes, you can have two! One each. It might stop you quarrelling!"

It didn't, of course. I don't think anyone could live with the Afterthought and not quarrel. She can be just *so annoying*! But most of the time, these days, we are good friends, and at least we don't quarrel with Mum. Certainly not like we used to. Mum still won't let me

read *Babe*, or stay out till midnight, or go to wild parties, and I still have occasional spats with her on the subject of clothes (*inappropriate*) or boyfriends (*unsuitable*), and the Afterthought still throws the odd screaming fit or goes into the sulks. But on the whole we would rather make Mum happy than have her mad at us, and one thing the Afterthought *never* does any more is use Dad as an argument. I can't remember the last time I heard her shout that "Dad would let me!" She now says that she hates Dad and doesn't ever want to see him again. Mum has tried to get her to be less extreme.

"What your dad did was criminally irresponsible, and it's certainly very difficult to forgive him for it. I'm not sure that I shall ever be able to. Not completely. But for all that, he's not basically a bad person. Just a weak one. He does love you both, very much, in his own way."

But with the Afterthought it is all or nothing. She says she doesn't care. "Titch would have *died* if we'd done what he said!"

It is quite true. We heard later that Dad's friend never did go back to collect the car. Poor Titch could have starved, or suffocated, before anyone found him.

We called the little stripey one Tiger. Tiger and Titch! They play together all the time, and sleep in each other's arms. Titch belongs to the Afterthought and Tiger belongs to me, but I think they love us both equally.

We had a postcard from Dad the other day. He's not in Nice any more – if he ever was. He's in South America. I can't imagine what he's doing there; he doesn't say. He just sends his love and promises that he will "be in touch". The Afterthought says "Not with me, he won't!" She says if ever she picked up the telephone and it was Dad, she would slam the receiver down. She was always willing to forgive him everything, until that moment at the airport. Dad really blew it. Mum says, "Well! That's your dad for you."

I don't know what I would do if he rang; I think I would talk to him. But I don't know what I'd say! I'm sure one day he'll turn up on the doorstep, trying to make like nothing ever happened. Because, as Mum says, that's Dad for you.

I still have my passion flower that he got for me. My beautiful tattoo has worn off, but I shall keep my passion flower for ever. It will always remind me of Dad.

# Pumpkin Pie

This is the story of a drop-dead gorgeous girl
called Pumpkin, who has long blonde hair
and a figure to die for.
I wish!

It's my sister Petal who has the figure to die for. I'm the one
in the middle... the plump one. The other's the boy genius, my
brainy little brother, Pip. Then there's Mum, who's a high flier
and hardly ever around; and Dad, who's a chef. Dad really
loves to see me eat! I used to love to eat, too. I never wanted
food to turn into my enemy, but when Dad started calling me
*Plumpkin* I didn't feel I had any choice...

0 00 714392 3

# Boys on the Brain

"What are you doing?" I said.

"I am trying," panted Mum,
"to - get- out - of - these - jeans!"

Hi there. I'm Cresta and that's my mum – thirty-three going
on eighteen. Me and my friend Charlie have great plans: finish
school, get the grades and conquer the world! We've taken a
vow – No Boys before uni, but it's not easy with the gorgeous
Carlito and Alistair around… And how on *earth* can I put up
with a mother who has boys on the brain?

0 00 711373 0

## "Hi, this is Mandy Small telling her life story."

I may have trouble writing, but I have no trouble at all talking!
My teacher, Cat, suggested I record my life on tape so
here goes…

I live with my dad, who looks like Elvis, and my mum, whose
idea of a special meal is burnt toast. Sometimes I feel like I'm
the grownup and they're the kids.

But now everything's crashing about my ears, and Dad's too,
as he's just put his foot through the floorboards. I'm trying
really hard not to become a total fruit and nutcase…

0 00 712153 9

# Skinny Melon
## and me

This is the diary of me, Cherry Louise Waterton,
and I am writing for posterity, in other words
the future.

And do I have a lot to write! Mum's just re-married, but how
*could* she marry a man called Roland Butter – what kind of a
name is that? He's a total dweeb who sends me coded
messages and calls me Cherry pie. Yuck!

I've got my best friend, Skinny Melon, to cheer me up but I'm
not sure if even she can save me from Roland and his
messages, or work out what Mum's big secret is…

0 00 712152 0

www.**fire**and**water**.com
Visit the booklover's website

# The Secret Life of
# Sally Tomato

A is for armpit,
Which smells when you're hot,
Specially great hairy ones,
They smell A LOT.

Hi! Salvatore d'Amato here – call me Sal if you must – and I
am not writing a diary! I'm writing the best alphabet ever. An
alphabet of Dire and Disgusting Ditties.

I'm up to two letters a week, and I reckon it will take me the
rest of term to complete my masterpiece. By then I plan to
have achieved my Number One aim in life – to find a
girlfriend. After all, I'm already twelve, so I can't afford to
wait much longer…

0 00 675150 4

www.**fire**and**water**.com
Visit the booklover's website